"Really enjoyed CAT. It has lots of tension, is fast paced and well written. The details such as the Native American lingo, lore, and cliff dwelling are interesting. The story is a page-turner, and I'm sure the book will be a best seller."
—Wanda Snow Porter, author of *Spurs For Jose*

"Your book (CAT) was another thriller. I enjoyed it very much. When's the next one?"
—Pamela Dozios, editor/writer

"CAT is the fourth of the Zack Tolliver series and in my opinion, the best one so far. If you loved the late Tony Hillerman, as well as Craig Johnson's Longmire series, you will love CAT. (It) is one of those rare books where you race through the pages only to be sad when the last one is reached. Hopefully I won't need to wait too long for my next Zack Tolliver tale."
—Barbara M. Hodges, author of *ICE*

CAT

R Lawson Gamble

First paperback printing 2016
Rich Gamble Associates
Cover Design Copyright © 2016 by Digital Donna
ISBN-13: 978-0692712450
ISBN-10: 0692712453

For mom, from whence the fruit fell

Thanks to Barbara, Wanda, Pamela, and Craig

CHAPTER ONE

Eagle Feather raised the mule's head from the blood-soaked ground. He looked close at the gash in the throat, saw the marks of large incisors from a jaw strong enough to crush the trachea. Parallel slashes in the mule's shoulders showed how the attack had come—the leap on its back, claws hooking deep, the reach under to grip the mule's throat in its mouth and hang two hundred pounds of muscle like an anvil under its neck. This was a good-sized mule, no easy job to bring down. From the look of things, this predator was unusually large.

"Mountain lion," the ranger said, with a grimace. "Same one's been killing our livestock. It kills, but doesn't eat."

The Navajo guide stood, wiped the blood-caked dirt from his knees. "It's a big cat. When did you find the kill?"

"The wrangler found it this morning around six. Called me right away. I came right out 'cause he was really pissed. This is the third mule he's lost to this lion in two weeks." He leveled a look at Eagle Feather. "Can you hunt it down for us?"

"You want me to hunt it?" Eagle Feather was surprised.

"We've got plenty of mountain lions here in Grand Canyon, never had this kind of trouble. There's lots of elk, mule deer, anything the lions want to eat. Never had one attack our domestic animals before."

"I can hunt it." Eagle Feather glanced at his watch. "It's had a four, maybe five-hour start. You want it captured, or killed?"

The ranger rubbed his chin. "No point in capturing it. We can't move it anywhere, if we put it in another cat's range one or the other will end up dead anyway. This one has developed a fancy for killing mules. He won't quit." The ranger glanced toward the stable. "Last thing I need, it finds its way back and kills again."

Eagle Feather shrugged. "Okay, we'll kill it. You want it?"

"No, no, you keep it. I don't like to see them dead."

Eagle Feather raised an eyebrow at that but said nothing. He looked at the ground around the mule, found a good cat print to study. He'd remember it for later.

The park ranger wrote something on a business card and handed it to Eagle Feather. "Just in case you're still on federal land when you kill it—this gives you permission. I'll send out an official contract for you to sign when you get back."

Eagle Feather shook the ranger's hand, walked away. He went back the way he'd come; past the small stable, neat and prim, around the corral, through a stand of scattered pines, the acrid smell of them pleasant in his nose, on to the large macadam parking lot where his truck, a rust-pocked '63 Ford pickup, sat all by itself. This killing the lion bothered him, although it shouldn't. Killing was his business. As an experienced Navajo hunting guide, he'd done plenty of it.

He opened the truck door, reached in, lifted his rifle from the floor behind the bench seat, and removed it from its leather case. He took a box of twenty .308 cartridges from the glove compartment, put them in a vest pocket. He sat for a moment, considering, then brought out his phone and punched in a number.

"Prónto, Eagle Feather. *Yá'át'ééh.* You asked for a chance to shoot a lion. I got one for you, a big one." He kept the phone to his ear with a shoulder while he checked the rifle. "Yeah, that's right. No, today, man. Right now. Move it or lose it." He chuckled. "I'm on the South Rim, east end, near Navajo Point. Drive up to the East Gate. I'll track it long enough to see where it's going, come over and meet you there. Say eleven."

Eagle Feather's pursed lips formed a soundless whistle as he prepared his gear. He felt good. When a hunt came along, life's concerns shrank to a reasonable proportion. He closed the door of the truck, put on his black reservation hat with the single eagle feather set at a jaunty angle.

He left the truck where it was, walked back at an oblique angle to the way he'd come, toward the corral. He cast wide of the kill, hoping to intersect the cat's tracks. It was easy walking, with very little undergrowth beneath wide spaced piñon pines, few leaves, sparse ground debris. Eagle Feather grinned to himself, wondering if the park rangers came out at night and swept the forest floor, it was that neat.

As he walked he studied each fallen tuft of needles, each tiny twig. He stopped, grunted. There it was, the cat's print. It lay perfectly formed on the soft earth, a full five inches wide, oval toe impressions clear as any illustration in a textbook. Eagle Feather knelt, traced the edge of the track with his finger, found it firm, deep. This was a big, heavy lion.

It was the imprint of the rear foot. He looked beyond, saw the front print crowded close ahead of the rear, natural for a cat. He set his direction by it, walked on and found more prints. The animal moved easy, deliberate. Eagle Feather thought back to the mule. Beyond the kill wound at the throat, nothing had been done to it. A lion usually drags its prey into thick brush, hiding it away to eat it at its leisure. That didn't happen. Eagle Feather guessed the cat was interrupted right after the kill, forced away by the arrival of the wrangler.
Yet it hadn't hurried off. It hadn't run up a tree. It didn't scare, just strolled away.

The prints led him into an area of brush. Behind it, he found matted vegetation where the lion had waited, hoped the wrangler would go away so he could return to the mule.

Apparently it gave up. After that the tracks led south, away from the canyon rim into deep forest. Eagle Feather trudged on, a half mile, a mile—then a surprise: the lion prints looped east, arced north, headed back the way they came. The return path paralleled the outgoing track, just a hundred yards from it.

Eagle Feather scratched his head. If the cat were a human he'd guess it wanted to check its back trail. Problem was, if it continued on it would trap itself between the park road and the canyon rim.

The tracks kept on. It didn't make sense.

When he came to the park road, Eagle Feather looked at his watch. It was time to go meet Prónto. He walked along the pavement back to the parking lot, climbed into his truck, and drove out to the gate.

He saw Prónto 's truck parked on the berm. The man himself, a tall, spare figure, leaned against the ranger's cubicle, chatting him up. Prónto liked to chat with everyone he met. People enjoyed that.

Eagle Feather parked and walked over. The two men watched his approach. "Prónto tells me you're going after that mountain lion," the ranger said. "I wish you luck, it's been raising hell with our livestock."

Eagle Feather gave a tight grin, shook his hand. "We should be done by nightfall, with the direction the cat went."

Prónto stood, eager. Brown-eyed, black haired, he was pure Navajo. Taller than most, he towered a head above Eagle Feather. He raised an eyebrow. "Let's go."

"Easy does it. We got lots of time. Go get your rifle and kit from your truck. I'll drive us over."

On the way, Eagle Feather spoke what was on his mind. "This cat, it's not acting like a normal mountain lion."

"No?"

"It shows no fear. The wrangler came along after it killed the mule. It didn't bolt, just walked away; calm, easy, just lay down and waited. That bothers me."

Prónto chuckled. "That all?"

Eagle Feather shot a glance at his client. "No, not all. I tracked him a mile or so south, away from the park, away from people. I expected that. What I didn't expect, he turned, circled back on his own trail like he was checking to see if anyone followed him."

Prónto stared at Eagle Feather. "Smart."

"Yeah, maybe too smart."

When they were back in the parking lot, Eagle Feather retrieved his rifle and a pack from the truck bed. He checked Prónto's gear. They walked along the park road. At the place the lion crossed, Eagle Feather stopped.

His instructions to Prónto were firm. "I want you to stay fifty feet behind me. Be ready to cover me, but watch your own backside. Lions attack—"

"I know, lions attack from the back quarter. I'll keep alert." Prónto gave Eagle Feather a curious look. "This one's really got you spooked."

No return smile. "There's something wrong about this lion. I've lived this long because I follow my instincts. That's something you gotta learn."

He led the way into the trees. They picked up the trail right away. The big cat hadn't changed its gait, trotted ahead like it had an appointment. The underbrush here was sparse, trees spaced out, thick gnarly piñon separated by wide areas of sandy soil. The terrain was level. Eagle Feather felt Prónto behind him, impatient. He motioned him back with his hand. His own eyes searched side to side as well as up ahead. The cat tracks kept straight on.

The ground sloped, piñon and juniper trees grew shorter, twisted by wind. The canyon rim was close. The cat's big pugmarks led on.

A breeze picked up, blew in from the canyon. It brought a new scent. Eagle Feather stopped, held back Prónto. His eyes worked slow, careful, left to right. A cat can hide in a few tufts of tall grass; you'd never know it was there.

Eagle Feather breathed out. There it was—he'd almost missed it. He motioned to Prónto behind his back, sank slowly to a crouch, kept his eyes on the clump of matted, gnarled tree branches that was a bit too dense.

His brain sorted an outline of the cat through the tangle of branches, crouched, facing them, tawny body almost invisible in the dense juniper. They were almost to the canyon edge. The cat was cornered.

He felt Prónto raise his rifle behind him. He'd shoot over Eagle Feather, a perfect unobstructed shot. Eagle Feather willed him to concentrate, take his time. Better no shot than a poor shot, and a wounded animal.

The rifle barrel was rock steady above him. The shot came, expected yet startling, a shock to his ear. He didn't expect the cry of pain he heard, the sudden burst of breath from Prónto as if he'd just been hit, nor the impact of the big man on top of him, crushing him down with his weight, pinning him with knees doubled back, rifle beneath him. Something large bounded over them, raced on.

At once it all came clear to Eagle Feather's mind. He had been wrong. The tangle of branches was not the mountain lion. The cat had stalked them from behind, attacked them at the moment Prónto shot.

Helpless, his chin in the dirt, he could only watch the blur of motion run off through the trees, on toward the canyon rim. He tried to move, felt the stillness of the weight on top of him. Eagle Feather now realized the enormity of his mistake.

CHAPTER TWO

She heard the cry one crisp October evening, her moccasins crunching on frosted earth kept cold all day in the shadow of the barn. Libby's gloved hand had just reached for the door's heavy slide bar when she heard it.

It was faint, far away. Had the wind still whispered in the treetops as it had done all day she wouldn't have noticed, but it since died. The dogs were quiet, too, almost as if listening.

She paused, waited. It came again, far beyond the pasture fence, up the wooded slope toward the higher elevations; a call of some creature, a wolf, coyote, maybe an owl, she couldn't tell. It didn't come a third time.

She shivered in the cold, pulled back the bar and swung the heavy door open. The dogs made their noise now, eager yelps and loud whines. A horse neighed, there was a whinny; a stomp came from the big bay's stall. Libby filled all the pans with water, poured out kibble, forked hay, strapped on feedbags. An hour later, she switched off the overhead light. Outside, she shouldered the door back in place, slid the bar home, trudged toward the house, her thoughts on dinner, the strange, far-away cry forgotten.

Libby Haddeford Whitestone-Tolliver learned to care for herself as a teen. Her maturity was thrust upon her, right here on the family ranch west of Cameron, Arizona, a place the Navajo called *Na'ní'á Hasání*. She was thirteen when her dad walked away and disappeared. Her mother, never a strong woman, simply gave up, left Libby to care for the ranch and her three younger siblings.

Any other young girl might have been overwhelmed, but Libby made it her challenge. She took over without missing a beat. Skinny, sun-freckled, spirited, she loved the ranch, the activities, and the chores—the tougher the better. Her father always encouraged her, even assigned a hired hand to teach her the skills a rancher needed. She got no favoritism; she got the same as any other hand, wanted it that way. Libby learned ranching through painful experience balanced by careful tutelage. She grew skilled in every aspect of ranching except roping. That's where her dad drew the line. "A girl's got to have all her fingers," he would say.

Libby loved her daddy, missed him terribly. Still, she rose eagerly to the challenge, just as he would have wanted, expected, almost as if he'd trained her for this moment.

Libby wiped the soles of her moccasins on the doormat, thinking how the years had rolled by since then. She stepped into the warm glow of the living room. A fire crackled in the fieldstone fireplace, its light danced on the rough-hewn ceiling beams. The savory smell of venison stew drifted in from the kitchen. Libby peered into the baby's room, still thought of it that way. Bernie looked up from his dump truck filled with wine corks, in his mind a load of lumber for the sawmill, gave his mom that brown-eyed soulful look. He had his dad's sincere gaze, she thought, for the hundredth time. She felt a pang, smiled at him, sighed and went into the kitchen.

Her husband was away a lot these days. When not on duty as FBI liaison with the Navajo, he was off dealing with unusual and unexplained crimes, consulting with law enforcement, suggesting procedures. His counsel was sought for unsolved serial killings and other murders where there were no clues to the killer. Libby teased him, said he had become the real life version of FBI agent Mulder in the old television series X Files.

When he wasn't off helping solve bizarre crimes, he was at a lectern talking about them, teamed with Susan Apgar, Chairperson of the Anthropology Department at U. C. Berkeley. Susan and Zack met in San Francisco when a fearsome serial killer stalked the city. From his actions, the killer didn't appear normal, seemed physically capable beyond the human race, perhaps a hybrid of some sort. Each reached this conclusion independently, from different perspectives: Susan theoretical, Zack experiential. On the lecture circuit, they made a convincing team.

They also made an attractive couple, Libby thought. The mental picture came unbidden, not for the first time. Libby felt shame worrying about such things. Zack had never given any hint of unfaithfulness; she doubted he was capable of such deceit—but the thoughts came anyway.

That night, long after Bernie was asleep, Libby lay in the large empty bed pretending to read a Louis L'Amour novel, her mind continually drifting from the page. She'd always been strong, but somehow the birth of their child made her feel vulnerable.

This was the time she dreaded most—when Zack was away and she was abandoned in the big bed, in the quiet house, alone with her thoughts. It had been years since her most recent night terrors; she worried they might start up again.

Fall was leaning toward winter. The cold weather was here, the bed sheets chilly to the touch. At this elevation, frost came early, affected her mood. When Zack was home at the end of the week, she knew she'd forget feeling this lonely, forget she ever doubted Zack and their relationship.

Libby snapped the book closed, snuggled down under the comforter, annoyed. She'd get by just fine, thank you very much. She always did.

CHAPTER THREE

Surroundings flashed by, luteous, veiled in a diaphanous green-yellow mist, indistinct, blurred; eyes were now ancillary, yielding to ears sharper than seemed possible, nose distinguished a hundred drifting scents. Exhilarating awareness, knowing where things are, what they are, steering, guiding, avoiding every obstacle, racing at great speed, leaping ledge to ledge, balanced, graceful. This power, this speed, this ability, *this excitement* was intoxicating.

The taste of blood in the mouth, a strange craving for more, compulsions undeniable, limbic system demands overpowering, human logic struggling to balance animal instinct, to fight the strong urges, understand their dangers.

A lightening sky; too close to dawn now, daylight impairing vision. Trapped between hunters and canyon, relying on animal cunning, a predator's appetency to ambush and kill.

Yee naaldlooshii, Navajo skinwalker, respected, feared, transformed, traveling as animal, highest level of witchcraft achieved only through sacrificial taboo, initiation into Witchery Way, years and years of practice as coyote, wolf, owl, mountain lion; building ever greater skill and power to the apex, the *náshdóítsoh* persona, the lion form, the Tiptoe Way, the height of stealth and swiftness.

Dropping into the great canyon, ledge to ledge, long leaps down steep drops, no hesitation, flying in a yellow mist like old sepia film, an eruption of muscle power, agility; all glorious, incomparable.

The cave, hidden, inaccessible, undiscoverable—there to begin retransformation, then recovery, time to reflect, consider mistakes, the hunters, the doggedness of their pursuit, the narrow escape, the crouched leap, long slashing claws, ripped human flesh, the report of the rifle. Saved by luck, by instinct—learn from the experience.

CHAPTER FOUR

The National Park Rangers evacuated Prónto to a Flagstaff hospital, took Eagle Feather's statement, and sent him off covered in his client's blood. As a courtesy, the rangers sent a copy of their report to Lieutenant Jimmy Chaparral of the Navajo Nation Police, a simple statement of the circumstances—a hunting accident, nothing more. Chaparral went to see Eagle Feather at his trailer. When he knocked there was no answer, although he was pretty sure Eagle Feather was home. He finally gave up.

Back at the office, Jimmy called FBI Agent Zack Tolliver with news of the accident, knowing he'd be concerned. He was. Zack didn't know Prónto well, had met him just a few times. The big Navajo was a good man, from all reports. Jimmy told him Prónto was almost killed, wouldn't be able to work for a long time. It would be a struggle for his wife and two children.

Zack's greater concern was for his long time friend Eagle Feather. Jimmy said the man was devastated; he'd never seen him like this. The Navajo guide took full responsibility for the accident, blamed himself; said it was his own mistake. He'd completely underestimated the mountain lion. Hearing this, Zack was worried enough to cut his trip short.

The FBI agent hitched a ride to Flagstaff on an Army transport plane, flew a small plane to the tiny Tuba City Airport. By the time his boots touched ground he was airsick—Zack didn't fly well despite pilot training and jump school. He signed out a Jeep CJ from the FBI pool, drove directly to Eagle Feather's trailer east of Elk Springs on a high dry-grass bluff among red sandstone buttes. At the terminus of the steep winding drive he climbed out, beat the dust from his jeans, and let his gaze absorb the deep azure sky beyond the creosote bushes and scattered dwarf pines dotting the mesa top. A slight breeze brought the scent of baked earth and dry sage. Zack took a deep breath, felt it in his lungs and heart. These were the sights and smells of home for him, always would be.

The trailer squatted nearby; its white painted aluminum chipped and scarred, weeds high around deflated tires. Two outbuildings thrust incongruously into the skyline—an outhouse with the usual weathered wood-slat walls, pitched roof and vent pipe, and a barn, once painted red, now faded to blotched mahogany, where Eagle Feather stored hunting and guiding equipment. No other structures marred the view—the man lived in complete isolation, liked it that way.

Zack leaned back against the jeep, arms folded, waited. He knew Eagle Feather would have seen the Jeep approach, would know it was Zack. If he wanted to talk, he'd come out.

Jimmy's call had been brief, yet worrisome. Eagle Feather lost a client; that was bad enough. He'd made a mistake, a misjudgment. That was worse. Zack knew his friend would have a lot of trouble getting past this.

CAT

The sun was warm for this late in the season; the breeze had a cool edge. It was ten minutes before Eagle Feather opened the trailer door. He came down the dirt path, slow, limping, like a hound returning to his master after he'd lost the scent. Up close, the Navajo's face was the usual blank slate, but Zack saw pain.

"Eagle Feather."

"Zack."

"I hear we got a lion to kill."

"Don't patronize me."

"You're the psychologist. I should try to manipulate your feelings?" Zack grinned. "Let's just go get the damn lion."

Eagle Feather didn't reply.

Zack tried another avenue. "How bad is that knee?"

Eagle Feather ignored the question. He spoke, soft, as if to himself. "I screwed up. I misjudged the situation, didn't understand that lion." The Navajo looked off over the sharp-shadowed glowing buttes. "I've never been so wrong before. Pronto paid the price, his wife and kids paid the price—my price."

"I get it. You fucked up." Zack leaned back against the Jeep. "I know you, we've hunted together forever. It couldn't have been all you. That lion must be smarter than most."

Eagle Feather's dark eyes met Zack's. He nodded. "Yeah, it's different." He seemed to see his friend for the first time. "You been home? You seen Libby?"

Zack shook his head. "Not yet." He stood upright. "I'm going home now." He climbed into the Jeep. "Like I said, I'm no shrink. I know this, though. Once that lion skin is tacked up on the side of your barn over yonder, you'll feel a whole lot better."

Eagle Feather stared at Zack, glanced at the barn, said nothing.

"Come by early tomorrow with your gear." The Jeep roared to life. Zack grasped the steering wheel, looked up at Eagle Feather. "We'll have breakfast waiting." He backed the CJ in a spurt of dust, wheeled it around and drove off. When he looked in the mirror, Eagle Feather hadn't moved.

At the end of the mesa access road, Zack turned west toward Tuba City. He pondered a stop at the office, decided against it, drove on to Route 89 and turned south. At Cameron, he drove west on 64 toward the Grand Canyon. The road climbed, pine trees grew thick, the air gusting into the open Jeep was crisp. Zack turned down an unmarked dirt road. Houses and barns peeked from behind pines at the ends of long driveways. A mile later the road ended at a red gate. Above it was a weathered crossbeam with Whitestone Ranch carved in worn letters. The drive beyond dipped, entered a valley, trees gave way to an open meadow bordered by a rail fence. A bubbling creek ran alongside the drive. The house and barn came into view around the next bend. Built of logs, the house was sturdy, durable. It had been hand hewn by Libby's

pioneer grandfather. Smoke ghosted from a stone
chimney.

As tires crunched stone, the front door flew open.
Libby stood framed there, watched Zack climb out, and
smiled. "You're a day early. I guess I can live with that."

Zack grinned, climbed out of the jeep and came up
the steps. He pulled Libby into a bear hug. "I got a good
reason. How's Bernie?"

Libby led inside. "Come see for yourself."

Bernie knew his dad's voice, came crawling toward
him on the polished wood floor. Zack scooped him up
with one big hand, hung him upside down amid giggles
and cries of "more, more". He obliged until the cries
slowed, dropped down on the living room couch, put the
boy on his knee for a pony ride.

"You have a good reason? Other than to see me?"
Libby pouted, settled into the adjacent armchair.

"You're right. I've got two good reasons. Well,
make that three. First and second, to see you and my little
cowboy, here." He bounced Bernie vigorously amid
whoops of delight. "The third is Eagle Feather."

"What's going on with Eagle Feather?"

Zack described the situation, as best he knew it.

Libby had known Eagle Feather even longer than
she'd known Zack. She'd been a widow back then, training
bloodhounds to hire out for search and rescue. Jimmy
Chaparral, with the Navajo Nation Police, used her dogs
from time to time to help track fugitives. Eagle Feather

often went along as guide. Libby's tracker dogs were well known and Blue, her best, was in constant demand.

When Zack arrived in Tuba City as an FBI recruit, he learned about Libby and Blue from Eagle Feather. He began to utilize her services. In a way, the three of them were bound together. Zack fell for Libby, married her. Naturally Eagle Feather was his best man, later became godfather to Bernie. After that, Libby saw it as her role to mother the confirmed Navajo bachelor.

Now it seemed Eagle Feather needed both of them.

CHAPTER FIVE

It felt good to talk to Zack, it always did. The man was direct, spoke what he felt, never had an ulterior motive. When he looked out the trailer window, saw his friend leaning against the Jeep with folded arms, Eagle Feather knew the stubborn agent wouldn't leave until he went out there. His friend had come because he was worried. He cared.

Eagle Feather also knew Zack wouldn't try to convince him to think one particular way or another. He'd try to help him, not with empty words, with action. Zack was probably right; hunting that lion was the best solution, not for personal revenge, not even for absolution—just to snap back into the present, get his mind out of the mire.

No one looked surprised when he showed up on Zack's porch early the next morning. An extra place was already set. The aroma of bacon and coffee mingled into an irresistible allure, a shaft of sun sparkled through the frosted window, the kitchen warmth beckoned. Eagle Feather felt better already. He walked to his place, tickled Bernie's ribs through his jammies as he went by. The boy giggled, pushed away Eagle Feather's hand. Few people knew Bernie was Eagle Feather's godson, or that he was named for him. Only a handful of people knew Eagle Feather's given name, or that he was half Jewish.

Eagle Feather sat down, grinned across the table. "How are you, Libby?"

Libby gave him a warm smile. "I'm good, Eagle Feather, really good. I'm always good when Zack comes home."

"Sorry to take him away again."

Libby's smile became a bit tighter. "He's home, at least, even if he's off on a hunt." She shot a glance at Zack. "I can live with that."

"Hey, I'm sitting right here, you know." Zack looked at Libby, concern on his face. "You never complained about being alone before."

Libby smacked him on the arm. "I don't tell you everything I'm thinking every minute." She climbed up from the table, went to the coffee pot. "Anyone want more?"

Later, as the two men drove off, Eagle Feather sent Zack a look. "None of my business, but it seems to me you ought to start picking up on Libby's signals a bit better."

"You get that feeling too, eh?"

"Just saying."

Zack changed the subject. "Where we goin'? Where'd you last see that lion?"

Eagle Feather grunted. "The last I saw of that lion he was running right at the canyon rim. I didn't track him then, I was a little busy. It's been more than two days since then."

"Into the canyon, eh? That makes it difficult."

"I didn't say it would be easy."

CAT

"Maybe I should turn back and fetch Big Blue." The dog's nose was uncanny; he'd helped Zack solve a long string of cases.

"I thought you and Libby retired him."

"Well, we did, but he's still got the best nose of the pack."

Eagle Feather shook his head. "I don't recommend it. This is a dangerous lion and Blue's an old dog. If it ambushed Blue like it did us, well..."

Zack thought of something else. "What if we catch this lion in the National Park? We can't shoot it."

Eagle Feather reached into his shirt pocket and brought out a folded piece of paper. "This gives us the authority."

Zack's eyebrows went up. "You let me think I talked you into this, an' here you planned to do it all along."

"I already had this," Eagle Feather said, putting the paper away. He pulled a map from his hip pocket, flapped it open on his lap. "The place I last saw the lion was east of Navajo Point. We can save time driving to the parking lot there and walk along the rim until we cut the lion's tracks. That way we can make sure it went down into the canyon."

"Sounds like a plan."

At the East Gate, they exchanged small talk with the booth ranger. Both men were well known to the park staff. The ranger refrained from asking Eagle Feather about the incident.

It wasn't far to Navajo Point. They parked near the trailhead of the rim path. A few cars were there, likely left by overnight hikers.

They left their gear in the truck. Eagle Feather led off, not moving as well as usual, Zack noticed. The knee injury still bothered him, apparently. Their progress was slow, both sets of eyes on the ground.

When they found the cat print, it was right where Eagle Feather expected. The Navajo had said the cat was large. Zack was still surprised by the size of the print. It was a good impression, large oval toes, distinct pad. The cat was running when he made it. There were no other good prints, but the signs were easy enough to follow to the canyon rim. That's where they disappeared.

Zack peered over the edge. "That's a pretty fair drop."

Eagle Feather knelt, studied the impressions. "It didn't hesitate, went right on over." He gave Zack a look.

"What?"

"This cat does nothing that is normal."

Zack grinned. "You got me fired up. Let's get down in that canyon and see what it did next."

CHAPTER SIX

The witch wakened, unsure of place or time. Reminders came with achiness all through the body—jaw, fingertips, back, knees, even arches of the feet, places seldom felt in human form. Sleep had been deep.

The *yee naaldlooshii* levered to a sitting position. The cave interior was dim. At its mouth, a shaft of morning light magically transformed the cave floor from sandstone grit to bright jewels.

Ravenous hunger overtook it. Memory came sketchy, unclear; more a hazy, sensory thing. There had been a kill—there had been an encounter with humans. The witch hugged its knees, rocked, chanted softly, waited for the past to come clear, to take shape.

The cave was empty save for a large earthen pot. Anyone coming upon it, unlikely as that was, would find it similar to the surrounding caves; unoccupied with undisturbed dust, a bit of scattered straw, an earth-toned cracked pot melded into shadow. If they entered, looked in the pot, they would find a fragment of animal skin, some herbs like windblown seeds—nothing more.

The witch's path to *clizyati*, "pure evil", a level of shamanism few achieve, a pinnacle of hate for fellow human beings of such intensity it froze the heart with its cold grasp like tundra enclosed in ice, had begun early. The child's road to witchery was destined; the blood in its veins flowed with a disposition for witchcraft from generations of necromancers. Schoolmates knew, feared, frequently abused the child for its heritage, as one might the offspring of a serial killer or rapist, yet in so doing eliminated any possibility of an alternate destiny. The young heart hardened. Acts necessary to progress along the path toward the Witchery Way became easier.

Memories returned now, images from the transformed state, flashes at first, then faster, unbidden, beyond control. The witch waited, collected them, let the human brain patch them together until a narrative formed.

The mule kill was good. It was clean, fast, a powerful strike against a strong animal, at least until the wrangler interrupted. There was the encounter with hunters, their pursuit. It was a mistake to attack the men. The humans would hunt the mountain lion in earnest.

The witch rose, moved on soft moccasins to the cave entrance. There would be trouble from this past night. People would buzz and swarm like bees in a disturbed hive, looking for something to sting. It was time now for patience, to wait for the hive to settle.

CHAPTER SEVEN

The trail into the canyon from Navajo Point was deceptive. It started out level for the first hundred yards then plunged. There were four by six boards every ten feet on the wide trail, meant to minimize erosion. They created an eight-inch drop every few steps. Zack saw how it aggravated Eagle Feather's knee, knew he would not complain. He studied the Navajo's hunched shoulders, grey streaked black hair tied up in a ponytail with colorful beads, the wide-brimmed black hat with its lone eagle feather. The man exuded determination.

The sun climbed. Zack slipped off his jacket. It grew warmer with each step they descended, the chill of October conceding to September warmth in the canyon depth. Streaming sunlight on canyon walls revealed infinite gradations of orange, red and yellow and set aglow the top of each promontory it touched. The sheer scale of the canyon took Zack's breath away, no matter how many times he experienced it.

After a mile or so the trail leveled, led along a ridge aimed spear-like at the canyon's heart a thousand feet above the chasm floor. They left the path before that, stepping onto the pristine, softly angled slope of the canyon wall, post-holing in deep, dry terracotta. Chunks of crusty red earth slid away with each step, threatening to unbalance them. It was delicate, difficult travel. Zack wondered about Eagle Feather, it must be hell on his knee.

Half an hour later the rising sun caught them. The heat was immediate. When Eagle Feather paused to rest, Zack found his water bottle. They drank deeply. Both men shed outer layers and packed them away.

Zack squinted up the slope. "How far along do you think we've come?"

"We should cut the lion tracks soon," Eagle Feather said. He shrugged. "Or not at all, if it turned off another way."

It hadn't. They'd barely resumed the trek after their rest when Eagle Feather stopped.

"There it goes." He pointed.

Zack saw where tracks crossed, angling along the slope.

Eagle Feather studied them. "It's moving easy, no hurry-up at all." He peered at the slope ahead.

Zack came next to him. The main canyon began its turn north here, the slope they were on continued into a side canyon. The cat tracks went that way, the hunters followed.

The slope steepened, balancing on the sliding earth wasn't easy, but their spirits were high now. The cat kept its traverse of the slope, left large depressions that were easy to see.

The sun burned hot as it neared its zenith. No breezes stirred deep in the canyon. Sweat soaked Zack's shirt, trickled down his chest and back. Eagle Feather's hatband was dark with it. They couldn't relax for a minute on this steep grade. If they fell, there was nothing to stop them.

The cat prints aimed toward a rock outcropping thrust up through the earth like a shark's fin above the water. When they arrived at its base, the tracks were gone.

The fine wasn't very high, maybe 30 feet. They saw by the deep impression that the cat had leapt up it. The men walked upslope until they could walk out on the top of it. The surface here was narrow, uneven, and rocky. The lion would leave no prints here.

The ridge did offer a fine vantage to study the ground ahead. The character of the side canyon changed, rock replaced sand, the slope steepened until it became a vertical wall. The only way to go forward from here was down.

"I think we can assume the cat went down from here," Zack said.

"How can you be sure?"

"Well, look out there. It's the only possibility."

Eagle Feather slowly shook his head. "I underestimated this animal once. I won't again."

Zack shrugged. "Its the only way we can go, anyhow." He grinned, looked at his watch. "Decision time. Are we going down, or are we going back? Will we be home tonight, or be home tomorrow?"

Eagle Feather was emphatic. "I came to shoot a mountain lion. That is what I will do. It was your idea, White Man.'

Zack stared down at the steep rocky slope they would have to descend.

"Don't stay for me," Eagle Feather said. "You must think of your family. Your credit is not so good with Libby, I think."

Zack grinned sheepish, then shrugged. "I got you into this, an' I probably can't piss Libby off more than I already have."

Eagle Feather nodded and began the downward scramble.

CHAPTER EIGHT

The *yee naaldlooshii* stood at the cave entrance, re-energized, warmed by the sun, thoughts on food. The cliff fell away hundreds of feet to the canyon floor. Soon it would be time to climb the ancient footholds carved into the sandstone to the canyon rim. The witch delayed, basked in the sun, always hesitant to leave this place.

The witch went rigid. A strange scent came to its nose, an unusual sound caused it to slide back inside the cave.

There, again—the scuff of boots on crusted earth, a loosed rock bounding, barely perceptible far away noises yet audible to sensitized ears. There were people in the canyon.

This was a surprise. People did not come to this desolate place. Whoever they were, they were not here by accident—they came for a reason. A wave of hatred surged, but logic prevailed. It was the consequence of the attack on the hunters. These people had come in retribution.

From the sounds, there was more than one person. A quick peek revealed two men, tiny figures working down the opposite canyon wall—they followed the lion tracks. One was the Navajo with the hat and feather. The other was a white man.

The white man was a concern. A white man had political power, could bring pressure to bear and bring a flood of hunters into this canyon. The consequences of the attack on the hunters loomed even larger now. This white man must be dealt with, and soon, before he could do damage.

The skinwalker went back into the cave to think. Perhaps this white man could be frightened away, but first he must be identified. Then a way could be found to deal with him.

CHAPTER NINE

Libby stared at the dirty plate and half-empty glass on the table, the sparse evidence that Zack had actually been there. A wave of bitterness swept over her.

Her decision to marry Zack hadn't come easily— she'd had to struggle with it. It wasn't because of her feelings for him. It was more the fear of losing her independence. For her, that was like giving up her soul. Libby had been married before, had chafed in the bonds. It had worked out, he was a wonderful man, but after he died she felt a guilty sense of freedom.

Zack reassured her, promised they would continue their own busy lives. They were older now, he pointed out, and both had careers. They'd just continue on, live separate lives each day, and join together each night—the best of both worlds.

He'd been right. Zack reported to the FBI office in Tuba City every morning, or went out on the Rez somewhere. She kept busy training her dogs, working with clients, running the ranch. True, there were nights one or the other had to be away, but those times were infrequent, and when they were together again, they had that much more to talk about.

When this arrangement had come to an end, it was nobody's fault. It ended because of a great gift, the birth of their son. Libby dropped many of her best clients then, turned over much of the ranch work to a hired hand and spent her days with the baby. Zack continued to work, of course; they needed his income. But that was all right too, for now they had little Bernie to share each night.

The change came after Zack met Susan Apgar while working a case in San Francisco. She was an anthropology professor with a pet theory about the existence of an alternate species of humans, a notion that dovetailed with some of Zack's ideas born of unexplained circumstances he'd experienced on the reservation. They became kindred spirits, excited by the similarity and verisimilitude of their belief, willing to proselytize at every opportunity. From that time forward, Zack was on the road constantly, always off on the lecture circuit with the attractive Dr. Apgar whenever his work would permit, leaving Libby at home by herself to care for their child.

She moved around the table gathering dirty dishes. It was ironic that Zack had dropped everything to come home, not for her or Bernie, but for Eagle Feather, to help him with his feelings. What about her feelings? They didn't seem to rate as high with Zack anymore.

Libby rinsed the plates, dumped them in the dishwasher, keeping one ear tuned for Bernie's little voice in his bedroom where he played. She had been so excited to see Zack and then off he went on this mountain lion hunt with Eagle Feather for who knows how long, with hardly a word for her. She had said nothing, didn't want him to think her petty or a nag.

Libby was caught up in her thoughts when the sound of knocking intruded. How long had that been going on? When she swung the door open her face was flushed as much with embarrassment about her thoughts, as from the heat of the kitchen. The tall slender man stood on her porch, amusement in his brown eyes.

"I didn't know how long you were going to make me pound on your door," Jimmy Chaparral said.

"Oh, I'm so sorry, I was caught up in my work."

He flashed white teeth. "May I come in?"

Libby was still suspended between two worlds. "Uh, sure...yes, of course." She swung the door wide.

Jimmy came in. "You look especially attractive this morning, Libby, kind of all aglow. You must be glad to have Zack home."

His words made Libby flush even more. "Well no, actually, that's not...well, yes, of course."

Jimmy looked closely at her. "Are you okay?"

Libby now flushed with annoyance. This flustered little woman bit was not her thing, and she was not happy to give that impression, especially to Jimmy.

At the sound of voices, Bernie made his appearance. As the little boy crawled toward him, Lieutenant Chaparral scooped him up. They were old buddies.

"I came to see Zack, actually, but I see his truck is gone and Eagle Feather's is here..." He gave Libby an inquiring look, put the squirming boy back on the floor. He sat down on the sofa.

Libby's smile was dour. "Yes, they're off to hunt that lion."

Jimmy gave a soundless whistle. "I knew Zack could stir Eagle Feather out of his malaise, if anyone could."

"If the man suffered from any malady, you couldn't tell by the breakfast he just ate."

Jimmy gave a hearty laugh. "Well, that's the best news yet." He grinned at Bernie who appeared startled by the sudden sound of the laughter, patted the boy on the head. "Never knew Eagle Feather not to be up for a hunt."

"Can I get you a coffee? We've half a pot left."

"Excellent. I'd love a cup."

Libby continued their conversation through the open doorway. "Speaking of hunting," she said, pouring his coffee, "you bring to mind a sound I heard the other evening, some sort of animal cry. It was strange to me, I don't believe I've heard it before."

Jimmy raised his eyebrows. "What sound was that?"

"Well, I wouldn't mention it, but you know this area as well as anybody. We both were raised here. But that sound...it came twice, when I was on my way to the barn a few nights ago. I've not heard it since. I wouldn't even mention it but it was so strange." Libby had turned toward him with the coffee mug, stopped mid sentence, startled by the look on Jimmy's face.

"Go on." Jimmy leaned forward.

She handed him the mug. "Well, that's it, there's nothing else. Just that sound."

"What was it like?"

"It was a call, like a wolf, but not so drawn out, not the same voice, but—" Libby shook her head. "I'm not explaining myself very well. I guess I'm a little off this morning."

"No, no, that's fine. How far away was it? What direction?"

"It seemed quite distant. It was difficult to tell the direction, but from here it seemed off to the northwest."

"Toward the Canyon?"

"Uh, yeah, more or less." She watched Jimmy's face. "Why?"

The policeman's features relaxed into a smile. "Oh, nothing. You know how talk gets started on the Rez. There's been some buzz about a predator in the area. Some sheep were killed, someone's dog was attacked, that kind of thing."

"Maybe this lion?"

Jimmy nodded. "Quite likely the lion. Now that Zack and Eagle Feather are on its trail, we can cross that concern off our list."

Libby looked carefully at Jimmy. She'd known him a long time, long enough to know when he wasn't telling all. "What are they saying about it?"

Jimmy looked embarrassed. "You know how people become when creatures attack their animals, or create a ruckus at night."

"Witches and skinwalkers."

Jimmy laughed. "Exactly. It's never just a rogue predator, it must always be imbued with an evil spirit of some sort."

Libby watched him. "Yet you are concerned."

"You know me too well. Fact is I'm always concerned when we get reports of skinwalkers or other manifestations of witches. The trouble never comes from some evil entity, it always comes from panicked citizens who grab their shotguns and act rashly."

Jimmy stood, put down his half finished coffee. "I've got to go." His expression was warm. "There's nothing to worry about, especially with Zack and Eagle Feather on the hunt. Just keep the animals close the next couple of nights."

Libby walked him to the door. "And if I hear that sound again...?"

"Call me right away. I'll come sit on your porch with my shotgun until I know you're safe." Jimmy grinned, put on his hat, tipped it to her, and loped down the steps.

Libby closed the door, stood for a moment, and smiled. She was perfectly capable of sitting guard with her own shotgun, as Jimmy well knew, but the thought of a handsome young policeman on her porch ready to defend her was, well, kind of nice.

CHAPTER TEN

"I just don't get it," Zack said. "We know the cat should have come this way, but there's no sign." He scuffed the earth next to the dry creek bed with his toe.

Eagle Feather didn't reply. He looked puzzled.

Zack gazed up the steep rock gradient they had just descended. "Maybe it's got a lair up there somewhere."

Eagle Feather's gaze went to the canyon wall opposite them. It was vertical, sheer from the base the first hundred feet to an overhang of smooth sandstone streaked with desert varnish. It was impossible for man or beast to climb. Above the overhang were horizontal layers of shale, with fissures and shelves where it was exposed to the wind, climbable if you could get there. Higher yet, as far as vision permitted, the wall was of limestone pocked with caves.

The Navajo guide crossed the creek bed, his eye on the dry mud bank. He stood, hands on hips, and stared up the sheer wall once more.

Zack joined him. "You don't think...?"

Eagle Feather pointed high up the cliff. "If I were a lion, I'd hole up in one of those caves way up there."

Zack squinted up at them, shook his head. "It would have to get there first. Even if it could climb this, it would have to cross this canyon bottom." He waved an arm at it. "Obviously, it didn't."

Eagle Feather shook his head. "We must have lost it along the way somewhere."

"That's the only thing makes sense."

Eagle Feather continued to study the caves. "My gut tells me it's up there, my brain tells me no way. I agree it had to cross this bottom somewhere, assuming it can't fly."

He glanced around. "Let's set up camp here. We can make a thorough search up and down the canyon to be sure the lion didn't come this way. Work for you?"

Zack nodded. "Sounds like a plan."

They made their camp high enough to avoid flash floods, tucked in close to the sheer cliff face. When camp was set, they went on their search. Zack went upstream, Eagle Feather went down the canyon. Afternoon turned to evening, but no luck.

Darkness came early in the deep canyon. Once shadows foretold the vanishing sun, the two dispirited men went back to camp.

Eagle Feather dug out his water bottle. "Apparently the lion can fly after all."

Zack shrugged. "Nothin' to do now but get a good night's sleep. We can take another look in the morning, when the angle of light is different. Sometimes, that's all it takes."

"If that doesn't work, this will be a short hunting trip," Eagle Feather said.

In the shadow of the wall, they made a small fire with dry branches, kept it just large enough to chase away the chill of the desert night. The sand was cool and soft under their sleeping bags. Even before the sun had gone, stars appeared with startling clarity, increased in abundance until they seemed to light the canyon with their brightness.

The two friends had plenty to talk about, they saw each other infrequently these days. The strenuous day took its toll, though, and conversation soon trailed off into sleep.

Zack was awakened from a vivid dream by sudden impact on his chest. He felt something moving. He raised his head to look, heard a distinctive rattle. He froze.

"Don't move, Zack." Eagle Feather's flashlight illuminated the snake coiled on Zack's chest, head drawn back to strike. A stick came into focus. The snake's head turned to meet this new threat, the stick went under it, lifted the snake. The rattler flew off into the darkness, impacted with a thud yards away. The flashlight beam came back to Zack's face.

"Did it bite you?"

"Jesus!" Zack sat up. All his limbs trembled with adrenalin. "Where did that come from?"

"That's a good question. It looked like a Grand Canyon Rattlesnake, sandstone colored with light bands, but I don't think it belongs at this elevation. They tend to live higher up."

"The way it felt when it landed on my chest, it had just been higher up." Zack climbed out of his bag. He took long, deep breaths. "How'd you happen to be awake?"

"I sleep light." Eagle Feather broke the stick, threw it in the embers along with several dry branches, coaxed the fire back to flame. The nearby sagebrush danced in the light.

Zack stared up toward the overhang. "I suppose it might simply have lost its grip and fallen."

"Seems unusual, particularly to land right on top of you." Eagle Feather studied the sand nearby with his flashlight. He gave it up, sat down on his bag. "Nothing there but our own footprints. It didn't crawl onto you."

Zack stood, picked up his bag, walked to the other side of the fire.

"Where you going?"

"Far away from that cliff in case something else falls off tonight." He threw down his bag and climbed in. "Good night."

When the first shaft of sunlight peeked over the eastern rim and lit up the tops of the towering castle-like walls, Zack heard Eagle Feather climb out of his bag. He pried open an eye and watched him walk out to the creek bed. Zack leaned on an elbow in the warmth of his bag, comfortably drowsy.

At last he willed his way out, threw wood on the fire, put a packet of instant coffee in two cups and waited for a small pot of water to boil.

Eagle Feather came back, as if drawn by the suggestion of coffee. Every line of his body sagged in disappointment. "It is no good, I can find no trace of that lion." He picked up a coffee cup, poured in the boiling water.

"Maybe because there isn't any, maybe because the lion never came down here."

Eagle Feather didn't bother to respond. He took a tiny sip of the hot liquid. His mood changed. He looked at Zack. "Not bad, White Man, considering it's instant." The Navajo leaned back on his elbows, looked up at the cliff face.

The cliff face took on new life in the morning, Zack thought, the dark streaks of mirror-like desert varnish glowed, bands of muted oranges, yellows, and tans suffused with the pink from the early sun. Higher up, stark shadows lurked in the caves, took on shapes, each a little different.

Zack watched Eagle Feather. "If the cat is up there, it had to come across here. I think we can both agree that didn't happen."

"It is up there, I know it." Eagle Feather looked at Zack. "What you say is reasonable and logical. It is time to wrap it up and go home. I will have to tell the rangers we did not find the cat and it might come back. Tonight I will stake out the mule corral. Whatever happens, I will not allow the cat to take another mule."

The men struck camp. Their movements were reluctant. After they dumped sand on the fire, they began the long arduous climb out the way they had come. Each time they paused to rest, Eagle Feather's eyes went to the cliff and the caves, studying them one by one. "I know it is there," he would say.

CHAPTER ELEVEN

The screen door groaned, slapped shut behind Zack. He strode into the small office.

Lieutenant Jimmy Chaparral looked up from his cluttered desk. "Hello, Zack."

"Jimmy."

Jimmy rose to his feet, came around the desk to shake Zack's hand. "Last I heard you were after a lion with Eagle Feather. Is the hunt over already?"

"Yeah, the hunt's over, the lion lives on."

Jimmy's eyebrows rose at that. He pulled a chair close to the desk for Zack, dropped back into his own, pivoted toward him. "You didn't get the lion?"

"Nah. We lost its trail. Eagle Feather is fit to be tied, as you can imagine."

Jimmy's eyes were wide. "I sure can. Where is he now?"

"He's at the mule corral on the South Rim. He plans to sit up there tonight in hopes the lion will come back."

"You think it will?"

"No, I don't. This cat seems to have pretty good instincts, it isn't gonna walk into a trap." Zack gazed around the tiny office. Not long ago this Navajo Nation Police substation bustled with activity, phones ringing, voices buzzing. They'd even had a receptionist, a Jill-of-all-trades who kept the place sorted. When she left to try marriage yet one more time, the tribe didn't bother to replace her. There'd even been another policeman; he was killed. They didn't replace him, either. The community of Elk Wells seemed to be melting away like spring snow.

Zack's gaze came back to Jimmy. "I got your message from the ranger and came directly here. I expect you didn't call me to talk about hunting."

"No, I sure didn't." Jimmy dropped his feet to the floor. "Libby probably told you I stopped by your place yesterday. I wanted to talk to you then, but you were gone. While I was there, Libby told me about an animal call of some sort she'd heard a couple of nights ago. She said she's never heard anything like it before. It bothered her enough she brought it up." Jimmy eyed Zack. "Did she talk to you about it?"

"Not a word."

"Right away it made me think about reports I've been getting, similar kinds of things; strange animal calls, unusual noises, even weird tracks."

"You wanna be more specific?"

"I can't, really." He jumped to his feet. "But I can show you. You got time to take a ride?"

Zack shrugged. "Why not?"

A few minutes later the men were in Jimmy's official truck, a battered white Chevy Blazer with the Navajo Police green and gold insignia on its side. They turned south off the main road. The truck bounced along a dusty track, in and out of occasional washouts. The suspension took a beating.

Jimmy chuckled. "Back in the seventies the department tried to downsize our vehicles. They thought it would be cheaper, more cost effective. Those cars were in the shop more than out of it. They had to give it up, go back to trucks like this. Standard police cars just can't handle reservation roads like this one."

Zack grinned in response. He looked out the window. "Isn't this the road to Sand Springs?"

"That's right. We're not going that far, though, just up on Tohnali Mesa a ways."

The truck spun wheels up a steep section. When the road leveled off, Jimmy cranked up the speed. A billow of red dust bloomed behind them. Ten minutes later, he steered onto a two-rut track headed west.

Jimmy glanced at Zack. "You know this road?"

"Doesn't this lead to the pipeline?"

"Yes, it is used by the oil company. You probably don't get back here much, it's to hell and beyond."

Zack shook his head. "No, not much."

The track climbed over ridges, dropped into arroyos, tilted the truck at crazy angles, at other times stretched out long and flat like a runway. They arrived at the pipeline. The road turned to parallel it, leveling out. They raced west another several miles to an even smaller track, just two ruts through tall grass.

Zack sensed they must be close to the cliffs, the great Adeii Eechii Cliffs that define the western edge of the Moenkopi Plateau. "Aren't we on the Hopi Reservation?"

Jimmy shook his head. "No, we're just south of it.

CAT

An arroyo developed to the left of the track, deepened until it fell away out of sight. The top of a dwelling came into view, grew into a traditional six-sided hogan made of mud and rocks. Near it the ground sloped away to the cliffs, beyond that, a vista without end.

"The Adeii Eechii Cliffs." Jimmy said. "Out there, the Painted Desert."

Zack was awestruck. Despite his long years of service on the Navajo Reservation, he'd never been to this place at the top of the cliffs. The view was incredible. "Whoever lives in that house has found a special place," he said.

"She's kind of a special person. She's the reason we've come out all this way."

The Blazer skidded to a stop a short distance from the hogan, next to an old GM pickup. The men stayed in the truck, waited to be recognized from the house. They didn't have to wait long.

The door flung open. A figure in a brightly colored shirt, blue jeans, wide-brim hat, rifle cradled over an arm, stepped out and stared.

"State your business," the intimidating person said, voice low.

Zack couldn't see a face; the hat brim cast a shadow. "This guy doesn't seem to want us here," he said, when the rifle tipped toward them.

Jimmy chuckled. "This guy is a she." He slowly opened his door, stepped out with empty hands in sight. "Do we have to go through this every time, Emma?"

Emma didn't move. "Can't tell it's you sittin' in there, can I? Who's that you got with you?" Her tone was harsh, suspicious.

Zack stepped out in the same manner as Jimmy, hands in sight. "I'm Zack Tolliver, ma'am, with the FBI. I'm Jimmy's friend."

Emma snorted. "Ma'am. I'm not your ma'am, not by a long shot—and a fed? James, what the hell is wrong with you bringing a fed out here?"

"Not just any fed, Emma. Zack is a guy who can help you and me with your problem. Give him a chance." Jimmy walked a couple of steps toward her. Zack figured Emma must have a fondness for the young policeman because she didn't blow him away on the spot.

"Go set yourselves down over there." She waved the rifle barrel at a log picnic table under a tree. She went back into the house.

The picnic table was set on a knoll just above the cliffs. Clouds layered the far horizon like a fleet of flat-bottomed ships on a painted blue sea. Each cast a shadow on the land below alternating with bright sun-lit desert, creating a checkerboard effect. The air was brisk, sweet smelling, the just-after-the-rain kind of smell. Near them, on the cliff top, the smooth sandstone was grooved and etched as if a giant child had scratched it with his knife. The hogan itself seemed to teeter above the abyss.

"I wouldn't want to be in that place in a stiff wind," Zack said.

Jimmy laughed. "That hogan's been there as long as I can remember. It's not going anywhere."

Emma re-emerged without the rifle, a plastic tumbler in each hand. Zack noticed she had a handgun strapped to her waist. Trusting lady. She put pink tumblers of water in front of each of them. They were plastic, the exterior scratched, ingrained with permanent dirt. Zack looked at Emma's face. Like her tumblers, her countenance was deeply lined by time. It was an austere countenance, with strength in the chin, and elegant, high cheekbones. She might be fifty—she might seventy.

Jimmy spoke, working hard to keep his tone light. "Time for official introductions. Emma, this is Zack Tolliver, my old friend and colleague of almost fifteen years. Zack, meet Emma Truewoman."

Zack smiled, nodded. Emma stared. He tried to break the awkward moment with a sip from his glass. "This is good water."

"Come with me." It was an abrupt command. Emma pivoted and walked toward the cliff edge without a backward glance. The men looked at each other, followed. Here's where she throws us over the cliff, Zack thought.

They went past the hogan, avoided the cliff edge, and came to a place where the ground sloped away into a large tilted sandstone bowl carved into the surface stone. It was partially filled with water, fed by a trickle from porous earth just above it.

"This is Tohnali Spring from the Navajo *to' naalini'*. It means water flowing downward." Emma pointed to a place beyond the pool where water ran toward the cliff rim and disappeared. "It's what it does." She turned dark eyes on Zack. "It is good water."

Jimmy coughed. "I brought Zack to hear your story, Emma. He has experience with unusual cases like this. He's often helped the Navajo Police."

Emma darted accusing eyes at Jimmy. "You want me to tell this white man? He is not Din-e'."

"He will understand, and he can help."

Emma kept staring at Zack.

Zack waited, became uncomfortable all over again.

After an eternity, she shrugged. "We will go talk to Amå."

CHAPTER TWELVE

Emma went into the hogan to announce them to Amå. The men waited outside. Zack was caught by surprise; he had assumed Emma lived alone. Five minutes later she returned and beckoned to them. They went in.

The house was surprisingly large. The interior was divided into two spaces by several large hanging blankets. The room they entered held four or five wooden chairs, the floor was dirt. Pictures of sandpaintings hung on the walls.

Emma put a hand on a blanket, held it closed while she gave instructions. "She does not speak English. I will translate for her." She spoke to Zack. "Her clients call her Amå—mother." She ushered them in.

An old woman lay on a low bed, propped up by pillows. A colorful woven blanket covered her. She was withered, etiolated, just a wisp of a person, her face faded mahogany. Her eyelids were half shut, just the whites showed. Zack realized she was blind.

"*Yá'át'ééh*," Jimmy said.

A bony hand rose weakly to acknowledge him.

Emma spoke a few words of Navajo then turned to the men. "I have asked mother's permission to tell you what she has learned. She will speak to you and answer your questions. I will translate." She motioned them toward mats on the floor. "Amå believes she is placing herself in great danger by talking to you."   Emma's stern eye went to Zack. "White man, Amå is a Seer. She uses *deest'ii'*, crystal gazing, to diagnose an illness. She is a Stargazer. Her mother taught her these skills, passed down from her own mother."

Emma turned entirely toward the men. "It works this way: a patient is referred to her, makes an appointment, as with any doctor. She discusses the symptoms with her patient to decide if she can help, then asks the patient to return at a future time. In the old days, when Amå was healthier, she constructed a sandpainting on the dirt floor before the client returned. She can no longer kneel to do that. But the painting is not so necessary; it simply represents Amå's particular star.

"When the client returns, Amå blesses the patient's eyes and her own with powder made from the lenses of certain birds. She chants and prays to her star to reveal the cause of the patient's illness and gazes at the star's light filtered through a crystal. Then she falls into a trance. Images appear to her, which she will interpret to understand the nature of the sickness. After her return she discusses the images with her patient, who may also have seen images. Finally, Amå renders a diagnosis based on her interpretation of all the images." Emma paused for breath.

Zack nodded toward Amå. "Isn't she blind? How can she..."

"How can she see her star's light? She says she sees it clearer now than when she had sight. The images are stronger. It is her power."

Zack opened his mouth to speak again.

CAT

Emma put up her hand. "Amå is very weak, but her fame has spread, and patients still come to find her. She does what she can. In the last months she says she has seen new sickness. She believes a practitioner of Witchery Way causes it. She feels the presence of *yee naaldlooshii*, a—"

"A skinwalker," Zack said.

"Yes." Emma's eyebrows lifted. "This sickness is caused by a spell. It destroys a person's synchronicity with the natural world. First her patients were confused, depressed, in despair. She was able to put them right. Lately her patients have come with swollen limbs, blackened tongues, and lockjaw. The witch's power has increased."

Emma's gaze was solemn. "She wants me to tell you this because she thinks you can help these people, where she cannot. The Witchery Way uses corpses. She sees all the symptoms of *'áńt'į*, that is corpse powder attacks."

"Can she cure those people?" Jimmy asked.

"Amå grows weaker, the witch grows stronger. She is less and less able to help these people."

"Why does the witch harm them?" Zack asked.

Emma spoke briefly in Navajo. Amå's response was weak and raspy. "She believes these people offended the witch in some small way. It seems to delight in its abilities. As it gains power, many people will be in danger."

"What can we do?"

Emma spoke again to Amå. After another brief interchange, she turned back to the men. "Your guns and

53

your laws won't help. You must locate the source of the witch's corpse powder."

"How do we do that?" Jimmy asked.

"Go to burial grounds, look for disturbed graves. Look for the corpses of children especially. If you find bodies missing fingers or the backs of skulls, it is the work of the witch."

Zack was incredulous. "Then what?"

Amå said something directly to Zack.

Emma translated. "Then you must identify the witch."

"How do we do that?" Jimmy asked, again.

"The witch uses the victim's clothing, or a body part like fingernail clippings. It will be someone familiar to the victims, someone who has access to these things. It may revisit the grave site, if you can locate it."

"I'll need a list of her patients, the ones who offended the witch," Zack said.

Emma gave him a look of incredulity. "This is not your world, white man. She can't give you that. Her clients are her sacred trust."

Jimmy turned to Zack. "People will know. The word spreads. I can get information from others."

Emma looked grim. "You need to act quickly. Soon this evil will grow too strong to stop."

CHAPTER THIRTEEN

Zack followed Jimmy back to the Blazer, his head
spinning. The dying sun made shadows stretch, tinted
everything a rose color Purple clouds floated on the
vehicle windshield.

"I understand your concern," Zack said to Jimmy,
as he climbed into the passenger seat. "But you know what
I'm gonna say."

Jimmy slid behind the wheel, sighed. "Of course.
We have nothing to go on—no crime, no victims, no
perpetrator. There is nothing for the law to act upon."

"There's precious little for anyone to act upon."

Jimmy tapped Zack's knee with a forefinger. "You
and I have different obligations. Your responsibility is to
uphold the law of the U.S. government. My obligations are
not so simple. I must enforce the laws of the Reservation,
and I must also satisfy the expectations of my people. My
people would say there is a lot to go on from what we just
heard."

"What do you intend to do?"

"I will visit every burial ground I can find
beginning with the nearest cemetery and keep searching
until I find a disturbed grave."

"Then what? You can't just grab a shovel and start
digging."

"No, I need permission from the Tribal Council to do that, but at least I will know where the suspicious sites are."

"When do you plan to do this?"

Jimmy glanced at Zack, his jaw set. "Right now."

Zack groaned. The men were silent, the creaking and groaning of the truck springs the only sound. As dusk eased toward darkness, depressions in the road hid in shadow. The ride got rougher.

After a time Zack stirred. "I'll help you."

Jimmy glanced at him. "No need. You should get home."

"I can't leave you to do this alone. There are a lot of burial sites; it would take too long. Together we can do it in half the time."

"I'm not going to turn you down." Jimmy said. "None of my business, but is everything alright between you and Libby?"

Zack answered the question with a question. "Where do you intend to start?"

"Not sure—maybe at the Tuba City Community Cemetery, after that, the old Latter Day Saints Mission graveyard. I've heard there are some new graves there. It gets harder after that. There could be isolated graves almost anywhere from old traditional burials. Most other organized cemeteries are at least 50 miles away—rather inconvenient for our corpse seeker, I would think." Jimmy downshifted, looked at Zack. He smiled. "First things first, though. Let's head over to Julia's Diner and get some dinner. We might even pick up some interesting gossip while we're there."

Zack looked at his phone—no signal. He'd have to remember to try Libby later.

By the time to two law officers walked out of Julia's, contented and full, it was dark.

Jimmy lifted his collar against the chill. "This might not be the best time to wander around graveyards."

"If anyone has the authority, we do." Zack chuckled. "I know what you mean, though. We could meet people who no longer recognize our authority." He glanced sidelong at Jimmy.   The Navajo ignored his attempt at humor.

It was not far to the Community cemetery, just a bit beyond the Quality Inn, up the road on a high slope. The men climbed out, stretched.

"The graves here are mostly within plots enclosed by a chain-link barrier. The plots are scattered around the cemetery." Jimmy reached into the back of the truck for a knapsack. He brought out two large flashlights, gave one to Zack. "I suggest we cross over to the far side of the property to begin our search. A disturbed grave there is less likely to be noticed."

Except for the weather-beaten wood sign that named it, one wouldn't know a cemetery was here at all. Greasewood and clumps of sage dotted the knoll and effectively hid the individual plots. The men had to keep their torches aimed at the ground, alert for rattlesnakes. They passed many enclosed gravesites along the way, some well kept, others overgrown. A loud flapping sound startled Zack until his flashlight beam found an American flag caught by a gust of wind.

Jimmy stopped on the far side of the knoll. Zack saw him search with his light here and there among the greasewood. "We should search for graves outside cordoned plots," he said. "There will be a few—drifters, unknown persons. A witch would look for those."

"Emma mentioned a preference for children. Aren't they most likely to be in a protected plot?"

"You're probably right, but there were some children without families buried in the old days. They might be in solitary locations."

The men divided up, searching independently, their flashlight beams darting here and there. After a thorough search of the far side of the hill, they worked their way back toward the cemetery entrance.

The search went faster, most of the graves in this location were well kept, visible with a quick sweep of the light beam. Nothing appeared disturbed. An hour later, they stood together next to the Blazer. They spoke softly now, as if influenced by the ground they trod.

"No luck."

"I suppose we should consider that a good thing," Zack said.

"Not if we really want to stop this witch."

"You really think you can connect some old man gnawing on bones in a hogan somewhere with one of Amå's black tongued patients?"

"My job is to follow the trail. If I find something to act upon in my law enforcement capacity, I will. If all I find is a name, I will turn it over to the tribal elders and wait for their decision."

Zack shrugged. "Okay, where next?"

"The old mission graveyard."

"The Mormon Cemetery? Isn't that on the Hopi Reservation?"

"Yes, it is."

"You have no jurisdiction there."

"That's where you come in." Jimmy grinned and climbed into the driver seat. The truck roared to life, its lights stabbed the darkness. They drove south down Main Street.

Zack glanced out the window at the bright lights of the combination filling station/gift shop, looked back at Jimmy. "You know, I have no real jurisdiction on either reservation. If someone catches us wandering in that cemetery, we could upset people."

"Let's not let anybody catch us."

Beyond the interchange with Route 160, it was completely dark. Pinpoints of light indicated distant homes. A while later, they turned right on an asphalt road, took another right into an empty parking lot.

Jimmy stopped the truck, turned off the headlights. He stared at the windshield. "If someone discovers us and gives me a chance to explain, they'll see this as a common cause." He paused. "If they don't, we'll be ducking bullets."

Zack groaned. "That's pretty much what I suspected." They climbed out, flicked on their flashlights. The red surface of a nearby building caught their beams.

"That's the old mission church," Jimmy said. "They took down the steeple, now they use it as a daycare center. There's a trailer behind it, a family lives there."

"Caretakers?"

"I think so. Let's go see if anyone is home."

They found a path of packed earth around the daycare building. A pool of light beyond it led them to an enclosed yard, and the glowing side window of a trailer. A dog barked inside as they approached.

The trailer door flew open. A man blocked the light. He pointed a rifle pointed at them. "Hold it right there. Don't move." The command came twice, once in English, once in Navajo.

Jimmy held up a hand. "Hold on, we're police officers. We'd like to talk to you."

"Step close so I can see you. Show me some identification."

Jimmy walked through the gate up to the door. Both men dug out badges, held them up in the light.

The man kept his rifle pointed at them with one hand, reached out and took both IDs with the other. He glanced at them, kept them. "What do you want?"

"Are you always this edgy?" Zack's voice was soothing.

"Maybe I got reason to be. What do you want?"

"We're searching for disturbed graves," Jimmy said.

60

"In the middle of the night?"

"We just searched the Tuba City cemetery. Darkness caught up with us." Jimmy paused, added, "We have reason to believe there may be some urgency."

The man stared. He was young, probably in his twenties, wore glasses and had an earnest look. Zack guessed he must work at the school.

"FBI, eh? You better come in and explain." He lowered the barrel of the rifle, held the trailer door open for them.

They found themselves in a small anteroom, beyond it somewhere a TV sounded. A young woman held the hand of a small boy. His large brown curious eyes stared at them from the hallway.

The man motioned them away, made a sign to the men to sit. Zack and Jimmy shared a bench. Their host leaned his rifle in the corner near some gardening tools, gave back their credentials.   "What do you want?"

"I am Lieutenant Jim Chaparral, Navajo Nation police—"

"I know who you are. Says it right there."

Jimmy went ahead. "This is Agent Zack Tolliver, Liaison Officer to the Navajo Reservation. We are here on unofficial business, I want to make that clear."

"Okay, that's an interesting approach. What is that business?"

"As I said, we're looking for disturbed graves." Jimmy glanced at the recently vacated hallway. "We have reason to suspect the presence of a skinwalker, *yee naaldlooshii.*"

The man dropped onto a stool, his face went pale. "What makes you think so?"

Jimmy described their visit with Emma and Amå, then went back to the reports he received prior to that visit, the disturbances in the night, molested livestock, wolf sightings.

"I have feared this. I am Jacob Naha. I am Hopi, a descendent of the Mormon Jacob Hamblin." He waved an arm. "I stay here to protect the spirit of his missionary efforts, or what is left of them."

"The Mormon Mission Church and the burial ground," Zack said.

"Yes." An embarrassed grin crossed Jacob's face. "I do not always greet people with a rifle. There have been several disturbances here after dark. My family is afraid."

Jimmy leaned forward. "What has happened, exactly?"

"First it was the dog. He doesn't bark much, just occasionally when he senses animals about. I'd get up, go out, look around, and find nothing. It kept happening. I stopped going out after a while, figuring the dog had a problem. We just tried to ignore his noise.

"About two weeks ago, the dog barked like crazy. I tried to sleep. Then something banged up against the trailer. Hard."

Jacob's brown eyes were intense. "I opened the door to let loose the dog. He wouldn't go, he just put his tail between his legs, whined, and slunk away."

"Where is your dog now?"

"He's in the back. He won't come out when strangers come, it's like something broke his spirit."

"Did you go out to look?" Zack asked.

Jacob lowered his eyes. "No, I didn't. I locked and chained the door, secured all the windows. Of course, I looked around the next morning. I found the prints of a large wolf."

Jimmy nodded, matter of fact. "What else?"

Jacob hesitated. "This may mean nothing. In the last week I found four new graves at the far side of the burial ground."

"New graves?"

"Yes, newly dug in places where none were before. This may mean nothing, as I said. Some families who have no other means will sometimes "borrow" a grave site."

"Illegal burials."

Jacob nodded.

"Have you inspected them?" Zack asked.

Jacob stared at him. "I'm not sure what you mean. There's not much to see but a fresh mound of dirt."

Jimmy raised an eyebrow. "No headstone?"

Jacob shook his head.

Jimmy stood. "Anything else?"

"Noises from time to time, usually in the back area, toward the new graves. I don't go over there at night.

These people obviously do their burying after dark so they won't be stopped. I don't want to stop a bullet."

"Mind if we take a look out there now?" Zack got to his feet. "We won't disturb anything, just look around."

Jacob ran his tongue over his lips, looked from one to the other. Finally he put both hands in the air. "Sure, go ahead. Just don't get shot."

CHAPTER FOURTEEN

The supper dishes were cleared and Libby was filling the sink when she glanced through the kitchen window and saw the wolf. Dusk hung murky over the meadow, the rail fence and trees were just visible. The animal stood in the meadow, face toward the house, ears perked.

Libby had been to the barn, the animals were fed, everything tucked away for the night. She felt surprise, rather than concern. Wolves were not usual in these woods, but they'd been seen near the ranch before, more curious than threatening.

Maternal instinct made Libby glance at Bernie where he played on the living room floor. When she looked back, the wolf was gone. It had vanished that same instant.

Her eyes searched, the field was pristine, empty. Libby shrugged. The dishes won't do themselves, she thought, but when the last utensil was toweled off and put away, she checked the doors and windows, made sure they were all secure. She was uneasy.

Libby felt a wave of annoyance at Zack. There had been no word from him since he left on the lion hunt. Even when he was home, he wasn't home.

She read a story to Bernie, watched his eyelids droop, then tucked him in for the night. She settled into her comfy armchair with a book and a hot cup of tea to wait for Zack.

When she caught herself begin to doze, she checked her watch. It was growing late. Where was he? Libby fended off another stab of annoyance, re-opened her book, and re-entered the fictional world it offered.

She awoke three hours later. The fire was down, her small reading lamp the only light in the room. Libby realized she had dozed off; her book was on the floor. It was time for bed, Zack or no Zack.

She sat up, the old chair groaned as usual. There seemed to be another sound at the same time. She held still, listened. Libby knew every sound in the old home so well she no longer heard most of them. This hadn't been one of them.

She waited, listened until she felt silly, started to rise. The sound came again. It was a claw-like scratching on the wall outside the living room, near the front door. It sounded like an animal. There were plenty of raccoons around, not to speak of skunks and squirrels.

The scratching moved to the front door, sounded like long nails raked across the wood. This was something larger than a raccoon.

The sound became more insistent, louder. The scratching became carving, like a knife gouging the door surface repeatedly. It grew furious, frantic, like a wolf digging for a ground squirrel.

Libby was terrified. She grabbed the phone, pushed the speed dial number for Zack. His cell phone rang and rang. The rasping became pounding. She heard wood rent, splinter. At any moment she expected to see sharp claws come through the door.

Zack's voice answered. Relief swept over Libby. "Zack, you've got to..."

"I can't come to the phone right now, but if you'll leave a message—".

"Damn you, Zack." Libby hung up. She searched for another number, panicked, got it wrong, tried again. Eagle Feather answered at the first ring.

"Libby, is that you?"

"Eagle Feather, someone's trying to break into my house." Her voice was low, urgent. "He's almost through the front door."

His response was immediate. "Libby, listen carefully. Turn on your alarm system so it sounds. Turn on all your outside lights. Call 911. I'm on my way."

The door shuddered from the pounding and gouging. The switches for the alarm and exterior lights were on the wall by the front door. Libby was terrified to go there, but had no choice. She flicked the light switch, pushed the button for the alarm system. A loud siren went off immediately.

The pounding and gouging stopped.

The phone rang. "What's happening now?" It was Eagle Feather's voice in her ear.

"It stopped," Libby whispered.

"The cops are on their way. They'll come with sirens on. Stay on the phone with me. I'm coming directly."

"Okay."

It was a half hour before Libby heard a distant siren. The noises had not resumed. Once the alarm sounded, Libby went to Bernie's room. He was standing in his crib, eyes wide, at the edge of tears. She scooped him up, sat in a chair, held him and waited while the lights flashed and the alarm screamed.

After an eternity, the doorbell rang, a voice called out. "Mrs. Tolliver. Police."

Libby went to the door, opened it. Two burly Navajo Nation policemen stood on her porch.

"There was an emergency call for this location, ma'am. May we come in?"

Libby pulled the door wide. Her arm trembled despite efforts to hold it still. Bernie, eyes wide, clutched her shirt. The alarm screeched on. Libby reached over and flipped it off.

"What happened to your door?" Both policemen stared; one traced the splintered hollows with a finger.

Libby looked for the first time. Many deep gashes, fringed with scrapes and claw marks marred the surface.

"Something tried to get in."

The policemen glanced at each other.

"A bear, you think?" said one.

The other shrugged. "Could be. You stay with the lady, I'll go look around."

Libby felt shaky; her hands trembled involuntarily. She led the policeman to the kitchen, put Bernie, wide-awake now, in his seat, and put on the burner for tea. While the water heated, she explained what had happened.

When Eagle Feather arrived, Libby came to meet him at the door. The house exterior lights shone on his truck and the patrol car, blue and red police flashers whirled across the walls of the house and barn. The front door stood open, a policeman was examining it. Another policeman was seated at the kitchen table, enjoying tea and cookies. Bernie was there too, laughing, his eyes on the seated officer, who pretended to poke him.

"Libby, are you okay?"

Libby gave Eagle Feather a shaky smile. "Would you like some tea?"

CHAPTER FIFTEEN

It was black as pitch outside the trailer. Zack waited for his eyes to adjust. Jimmy's flashlight came on, flickered here and there across the uneven ground like a lightening bug. Zack aimed his beam at the ground in front of him. Headstones came into view from time to time; some, partially hidden by weeds, seemed to rise from the earth as if to block their way. Zack took care not to step on the hallowed ground they marked. The smell of musty earth joined the scent of mesquite and sage on the sweet night air.

Ahead, Zack saw Jimmy's beam stop, hold steady. He came up, added his own light. This grave was fresh.

Jimmy's voice was hushed. "We are near the eastern boundary of the cemetery. This is where Jacob said the fresh graves were."

"We're not after what people put into the ground, only what somebody took out," Zack said.

"Yeah, but new digging isn't quite so easy to see in a freshly dug grave."

"We can look for fresh footprints."

"How will we tell them from the people who did the burying—or Jacob's, for that matter?"

"I have no idea." Zack flashed his light around the grave. A thought struck him and he chuckled. "If the instructors at the academy could see me now—looking for evidence that a witch digs up human bones to make a medicine to help him cast spells that turn the tongues black in people he doesn't like." He looked at Chaparral. "What did you really expect to find?"

Jimmy didn't respond. His flashlight beam traveled, paused, came to rest on another grave further away. He went that way.

Zack stayed, crouched and inspected the ground. He found fresh footprints—sandals, a pair of boots, pretty much what one might expect. They were at least 24 hours old.

He heard Jimmy's soft voice. "Maybe this."

"Maybe what?"

"Maybe this is what I expected to find."

Zack picked his way past dirt clumps and cactus. Jimmy's light beam was on a fresh footprint distinctly outlined in the soft earth, the print of a large dog.

Zack knelt, traced it with a finger. "Definitely canine, too large for a coyote, too wide, I'd say. The toe length is uniform; that suggests a wolf rather than a dog. Still, it could be a large dog."

Jimmy's light beam moved. "There's more over here."

Zack looked, saw more canine prints muddled together. He moved his light over to one side, saw the fresh dirt of a grave, noted how small it was, the size of a child. A hole had been dug in the middle, loose dirt piled up behind it, as if an animal had dug there with its forepaws. Zack felt his hair prickle.

The men studied the hole. It was about a foot deep, looked as if it may have been deeper at one time before the loose earth collapsed back in.

They stared at it in silence.

Zack breathed out, ready to speak when his phone rang. Both men jumped at the sudden sound.

Zack grabbed it, answered.

"Zack? Eagle Feather. Where are you?"

"You wouldn't believe me if I told you."

"Zack, you better come home. I'm here now. Libby is upset. Something tried to break in tonight, some kind of large animal. The front door is all carved up."

Zack was stunned. He couldn't speak for a moment.

"I'm on my way," he said, finally.

~   ~   ~   ~   ~

Jimmy dropped Zack off at the police station in Elk Wells where he'd left his truck. In another half hour Zack turned onto the dirt drive to his ranch. It was dark but for the double cones of his headlights bounding up and down with the road surface. He drove as fast as he could, the truck wheels sliding on turns.

His first view of the ranch house fed his fear. It was a circus of lights among the trees. When he turned into the drive he saw a patrol car flashing red and blue. Eagle Feather's truck was parked, its headlamps left on, shining across the meadow. Every exterior light, house and barn, was on.

Zack brought the jeep to a skidding stop, sprang out.

The front door was part way open. Eagle Feather appeared there. "About time, White Man."

"I came straight here. What's going on?"

Eagle Feather met him part way up the steps, talked softly. "Libby's pretty shook up."

When Zack started to pass him, Eagle Feather grabbed his arm. "I want you to take a good look at the front door before you go in."

Zack went on up the steps, stared at the door. "What the hell did that?"

Eagle Feather's eyes were on Zack. "A large animal of some kind."

Zack rushed into the house. The interior was brightly lit, voices sounded in the kitchen. Bernie was in his chair, giggling. Two policemen sat on either side of the boy drinking coffee and eating cookies. Libby was smiling and bustling about, but when she saw Zack, her look was not a happy one.

"Are you okay?" Zack went over to give her a hug, but she pushed him away.

The policemen stood up, looking embarrassed.

"Thank you for responding to the call," Zack said.

"Just doin' our duty." The officer smiled, shook his hand.

The other said, "You got a real big varmint out there."

"I saw the damage. You got any ideas what did it?"

"A bear is my best guess; only thing large enough. Maybe it smelled the misses' dinner and got hungry." The policeman turned to Libby. "Thank you for your hospitality, Mrs. Tolliver. Now your husband's back, we best move on." The second officer grabbed a final cookie on his way out.

Zack followed the men to the door, thanked them again. He returned to the kitchen and sat across from Eagle Feather. Libby was at the sink, her back to them.

"I think you've got a problem," Eagle Feather said.

CHAPTER SIXTEEN

When the shadow crept across the old woman's face, she lifted her eyelids, exposed white, unseeing eyes.

"Who is it?"

"You already know." The voice was coarse.

The old Seer turned her head, listened. She stirred in the bed. "I thought you would come."

"You have meddled in my business."

"I must tell what I see."

"You and I are of the few who keep up the old practices." The voice came from her other side, surprised her.

She faced the voice. "I am a Healer."

"You are a meddler." The words came in a hiss.

Amå waited.

"You are a meddler who reveals secrets to the *belagaana*."

The voice had moved again.

The old woman tilted her head, searched with her ears. "I reveal my visions, nothing more."

"To the *belagaana*." Spitting the words. "To the FBI man."

Amå heard growing anger in the voice. She said nothing.

"You have betrayed your people."

At this, the old woman lifted her head from the pillow, matching his anger. "No, it is you who have betrayed our people. It is you who practice the evil that will destroy us all." Her head fell back to the pillow from the effort.

"Old lady, you grow more feeble and useless. Your time in this world is short. There is nothing left in it for you."

Amå felt her throat gripped by long fingers, like talons, like steel bands. Her eyes bulged, her face filled with blood, she stiffened, went limp. It was done.

CHAPTER SEVENTEEN

Libby glared at Zack. "I tried to call you. You didn't bother to answer your phone. I had to call Eagle Feather for help." Her eyes were cold.

Zack sighed. He felt the churn in his stomach that always presaged a fight with Libby. "My cell had no service." He paused. "Maybe you and Bernie should stay at the Quality Inn in Tuba City for a night or two. You'd be near my office, and—"

"I didn't even know where you were." Libby wasn't listening.

"Jimmy left me an urgent message. I went to straight to Elk Wells after I came out of the canyon."

"You drove right by here and didn't even call."

Zack squirmed. "I know. I should've called. My mind was elsewhere.

"Zack, you and your mind have been elsewhere a lot lately. Maybe you need to think about where that mind of yours really wants to be."

When Zack didn't respond, Libby stood, picked up Bernie and marched out.

Eagle Feather watched her go, gave a low whistle. "Nice work, White Man."

Zack rolled his eyes at Eagle Feather. "Your thoughts I definitely do not need."

"If you had called Libby, she might have told you about the wolf."

"What wolf?" Zack sent a sharp look at Eagle Feather.

"Before all that"—Eagle Feather waved an arm toward the front door —"Libby saw a lone wolf out in the pasture. It was looking at the house, then it vanished."

"A wolf."

Eagle Feather nodded.

"There haven't been wolves around here in a long time." Zack thought about it. "You know, I just saw a wolf track, a big one. It was next to a fresh grave in the Latter Day Saints cemetery, the old abandoned one. The animal apparently had been digging in a grave."

It was Eagle Feather's turn to show surprise. "What were you doing there?"

"I was with Jimmy Chaparral. He left that message because he wanted to talk to me about the predation at local farms. People have been losing stock and pets. He also told me about an animal cry Libby had heard." Zack shook his head. "Libby's right, I need to call her more often. I'm getting all her news too late."

"There, you see? You do have the capacity to learn."

Zack ignored the remark. "Jimmy took me to see a Healer, a Crystal Gazer. She lives out on the Moenkopi Plateau."

" You mean Amå?"

Zack nodded. "She warned us of an active witch in the area, one who uses corpse powder. That's how Jimmy and I came to be searching through graveyards with flashlights."

"You surprise me, White Man. I didn't think you believed in witchcraft, only alternate species of humans."

Zack grimaced. "I subscribe to bad people doing bad things. The wolf is quite a coincidence, though." He gestured toward the front of the house. "That carving on the door wasn't done by a wolf, unless it was a two legged wolf."

Eagle Feather raised an eyebrow.

"No," Zack said, reading his friend's meaning. "A human is involved in this somehow, a real person who wants us to think it is wolves and witches."

"Have you pissed anybody off lately?"

Zack gave a sheepish grin. "Just my wife." He changed the subject. "Any luck with that lion?"

Eagle Feather looked annoyed, shook his head. "No. I didn't really expect it to return. But if it had and I wasn't there, I would've felt even worse." He stood. "It's late. I was up all night. I'm going home, get some rest, then I'm gonna go get that lion."

Zack offered him the spare room, Eagle Feather declined. After he'd gone, Zack undressed and climbed into a bed that felt cold for reasons beyond the cold snap.

It seemed only minutes later his phone rang, although the clock said 6 am. He noticed Libby was gone from her side of the bed. I'm not forgiven yet, he thought. He felt depressed as he reached for the phone.

It was Jimmy Chaparral. "Zack, you better come out here. I just got a call from Emma. Amå is dead. Emma thinks she was murdered. I'm on my way there now." He paused. "Zack, are you there?"

Zack let out a breath. "I'll be there as soon as I can."

CHAPTER EIGHTEEN

The drive to the Moenkopi Plateau was long. The Navajo Nation Police had already rolled out yards of yellow tape at the hogan. Jimmy came to meet Zack at the Jeep.

"No question. The old lady was strangled. Her eyes almost popped out of her head."

"What about Emma?"

"She's pretty upset. I think she's scared, though it's hard to tell."

"Was she here when it happened?"

"No, she has at home in Moenkopi, came here early this morning. Found Amá dead in her bed. She called me right away."

Zack climbed out of the Jeep, stretched his legs. His eyes automatically went to the ground.

Jimmy noticed. "I already searched for footprints and tire marks. There aren't any."

Zack glanced at him. "Anything near the hogan door? On the dirt floor inside?"

Jimmy shook his head. "Nothing."

They walked to the hogan. A policeman stood at the door. When he saw them he saluted and stepped aside. It was one of the same guys who responded to the call at Zack's house last night.

Zack nodded to him. "You didn't get much sleep, either."

Inside the hogan, Zack studied the dirt floor. His eyes worked along the hard packed earth toward the inner room. Jimmy was right. The murderer had not left any prints.

Emma was at Amå's bedside. She glanced up as the men entered, looked away again. "You are too late."

Zack approached the bedside. "May I?"

Emma stared, nodded.

Amå lay on her back on the bed, her arms at her side. She looked peaceful, serene.

"Is this how you found her?"

"Yes. I moved her arms close to her side, that is all."

Zack examined the woman's head and neck. She had been strangled with such force her eyes bulged and the skin of her face was drawn tight. A red-blue bruise circled her neck, almost like a ligature mark from a hanging. Zack lifted Amå's head slightly, looked at the underside of her neck. He saw two gouges deep into the skin at each end of the long thin bruise. He put her head down gently, looked at Jimmy. "We should get her to the lab for an autopsy." He saw Emma stiffen at his words.

Jimmy shook his head. "Not gonna happen. Anything we need to do has to be done here and now, as non-invasive as possible. They won't let you take her. This woman is a revered healer. She will be buried and mourned in the traditional way. There will be no autopsy."

"Can I at least have our forensic people flown out here?"

Jimmy shook his head again. "We are lucky Emma allowed you."

Zack glanced at Emma. She seemed not to hear their conversation, here eyes fixed on Amå. He sighed. "Okay. I've got my camera in the Jeep, and some swabs. Let's get a digital record and swab as much of the neck area as we can."

Emma let the two lawmen do their work. She stood by the door, her features frozen. When they were done and had packed up their tools, she returned to her bedside vigil.

Zack murmured condolences on his way out, but Emma didn't seem to hear him.

Outside, Jimmy spoke to Zack, his voice suppressed. "It is most unusual for a Navajo to remain in the same house with a dead person. It is a true sign of Emma's devotion."

"What will happen next?" Zack still had hopes Linda might get a look at the body.

"There will be a traditional burial."

"What's involved in the traditional burial? Is there a chance Emma might change her mind?"

"Not the slightest. The burial will most likely take place this afternoon. We won't know where, except it won't be here. A procession of cars will take her body to a secret place. A horse will lead the way from there to the exact site. The mourners will follow on foot. We've had our last look at Amå."

Zack paused, looked at Jimmy. "What do you think is going on here?"

Jimmy looked at the ground, shifted his gaze to the cliffs and the Painted Desert beyond, aglow in the morning sun. "I think she angered someone by speaking to us."

Zack dropped his case in the Jeep. About to climb in, he hesitated and looked at Jimmy. "Did you notice those marks on Amå's neck? It's as if the killer encircled her neck with his finger and thumb and squeezed, driving the nails deep into her skin." Zack made a circle with his own thumb and finger to illustrate. "He must have long fingers and very long fingernails and he must be very powerful. It looked to me he might have collapsed her trachea. It takes impressive strength to do that with just a finger and thumb. A forensic doctor might identify how it was done, but that's out now."

"You said he."

Zack shrugged. "Seems likeliest."

"You will show the digital pictures to Linda?"

"Right. With luck, she might find some identifying mark from the killer's hand when we blow the pictures up."

Jimmy looked hesitant. "Listen Zack, be careful. We may be dealing with a practitioner of Witchery Way, someone who..." He saw Zack's expression and trailed off. "Just be careful, okay?"

Zack grunted, climbed into the CJ. "I'm gonna take this stuff to the lab right now. Let me know if you find anything else." The engine came to life and the Jeep roared off in a cloud of dust.

CHAPTER NINETEEN

Zack placed a call to Libby when he approached Tuba City. He'd left a note that morning, but knew it wasn't enough. Now the phone rang and rang. *I'm truly in the doghouse,* Zack thought, feeling miserable. He drove on to his office in the FBI/Navajo Liaison building.

The FBI presence on the Navajo Reservation was unofficial, a courtesy by invitation of the Navajo people. The relationship between the FBI and Native Americans has a rocky history, the Navajo hoped to enhance communication in this way. The FBI building housed a brand new forensic lab, the domain of Linda Whittaker, Ph.D., a Forensic Pathologist with a wide range of investigative skills, and to some an annoying manner.

Linda had been loaned to the Tuba City FBI office several years ago for a specific case. She proved so valuable, Zack's boss fought to keep her. Linda didn't want to stay, she'd rather work in a large city, but once the Tuba City FBI found a way to finance a beautiful modern lab, just for her, with all the bells and whistles, she changed her mind.

Other things had changed. Zack was now Senior Agent in Charge with a young recruit to share the load. He had more freedom to pursue cases as he saw fit. There would always be politics—the people above him at Prescott kept him in line, mostly by his budget. None of them ever came out here to look around, though.

CAT

Today the recruit, Alex Brown, was at the front desk. He looked up when Zack came in, flashed an eager smile.

Zack smiled back. "Busy?"

Alex shook his head, black hair flopping. The long hair was not to FBI standards, but Zack encouraged it, theorizing the more Navajo the boy looked, the more they might accept him. His brown eyes and high cheekbones helped his cause.

"Slow morning so far, with a little luck it'll stay that way," Alex said.

"Is Linda in?"

Alex nodded. "Just in."

Zack walked along the inside corridor, followed it to the lab. He pushed open the dimpled glass door, stuck his head around it. "Anybody home?"

"C'mon in, Zack. Be there in a minute."

He stepped in. The room was bright. Reflected light from high wattage bulbs glistened off sanitized aluminum and glass. Zack pulled a stool away from a steel table and set his kit down.

Linda appeared from a back room, stretching an arm into a white lab coat, saying, "Just got here." She was short, pear shaped with a permanent dour look on her round face. At first glance, she seemed better suited to cutting cakes than corpses.

"Got some stuff for you to take a look at," Zack said.

Linda looked annoyed.

"I know, I know, it isn't *stuff*." Zack grinned, his look impish. "I have swabs from a neck wound, I'm hoping to find foreign tissue. I'm particularly interested in this sample from a gouge, seemed like a fingernail puncture. Might be some of the murderer's skin cells there." Zack reached into his case, brought out the digital camera. "I took close-ups of the wound. I'll put 'em up so you can look, tell me what you think."

"What's going on?" Linda reached for the swab samples.

"Someone strangled an old lady last night out on the Moenkopi Plateau. Jimmy's ready to believe a witch committed the murder. Hence my haste to find solid evidence, before that thought goes too far."

Linda chuckled as she arranged the swab samples onto slides. "Good luck with that. We are in Navajo Land, after all."

While Linda set up the samples, Zack connected his camera to her computer, mirrored it with a large monitor on the wall. After flipping through some old pictures, he found the first one he'd taken of the markings on Amå's neck. He walked up to the monitor, stood close and zoomed in and out with the remote. "I think this picture confirms my suspicion the killer used just one hand, his right hand. I see no superimposed bruising or compression marks to indicate a second hand."

"A strong fellow," Linda commented, her eye in the microscope. "Whoa, here's something."

Zack swung his head to look at her.

88

CAT

"I have a tiny bit of residue from your puncture wound swab. It shows human cells, as you hoped. But there is something else here." Linda removed the slide, took it over to the mass spectrometer. She placed the substance in the vacuum chamber and set it to work.

"What are you looking for?"

Linda watched the screen. "Our fingernails are made from a compressed protein called keratin. That's what I was looking for in this sample."

"Well?"

"Well, I did find keratin, but this looks to me like beta keratin. So I'm doing further testing to know for sure."

"Okay, keratin, beta keratin, what's the difference?"

Linda mumbled, her face close to the computer screen as she watched the rainbow effects of the ionization. "Vertebrates, that's you and me, have finger or claw nails constructed from alpha keratin." She interrupted herself. "Aha!" She rolled her chair back, swung around to look at Zack. "Yep, I was right. This sample is without a doubt from the helix structure of beta keratin. Your murderer is either a large lizard or a raptor."

CHAPTER TWENTY

Jimmy Chaparral went directly to the Elk Wells police station. He dropped into his desk chair, pausing to let his mind roam. He knew he could rely on Zack to pursue the hard evidence. Those results would come along soon enough. Jimmy needed to go another way.

Amå's murder confirmed his suspicions beyond doubt; there was an active practitioner of Witchery Way in the area. The lost and mutilated pets and stock, the ravaged infant grave, the strange animal calls Libby heard, her wolf sighting, the claw marks on her door, and now the killing of a Seer, one who might have used her powers to identify the witch. It all added up.

Now what? There were more than 9000 people living in the environs of Tuba City alone, another thousand in Moenkopi, and no way of knowing how many more lived in isolation elsewhere in the area. Jimmy decided to begin by plotting the reports of suspicious incidents on a map and see where that left him. He was hard at it when the screen door creaked open. It was Eagle Feather.

"*Yá'át'ééh.*"

"*Aoo' yá'át'ééh.*" Jimmy pushed the map to the side. "What brings you here?"

"I believe my purpose is similar to yours," Eagle Feather said, gesturing toward the map.

Jimmy's smile was sheepish. "I seek a witch."

CAT

Eagle Feather grinned. He pulled over a chair from the next desk. "With geography?"

"Yeah."

"How's that going?"

Jimmy centered the map on the desk, flattened the section for Tuba City, Elk Wells and Moenkopi. "I've isolated some of the recent complaints of livestock mutilations, missing pets, noises in and around houses at night, that kind of thing. I thought I might detect a pattern."

Eagle Feather looked at the map. "Seems like you did." He pointed out the group of red dots clustered north of Tuba City.

Jimmy nodded. "The greatest activity seems to be in the vicinity of Moenave, even a bit north toward the spring and east near the junction."

Eagle Feather studied the map. "Have you responded to all those calls?"

Jimmy laughed. "Oh, no way. There're always some crank calls, others turn out to be normal predation. I mostly handle calls by telephone. I did go out on a couple."

"Why those in particular?"

"One of them, I knew the people, they aren't alarmists. The other, the complaint was so bizarre I had to go and see for myself." Jimmy leaned back, grinned at Eagle Feather. "This is just a normal day at the office for me, you know."

Eagle Feather grunted. "I see other dots, one here, one over there." He pointed.

"Yeah, those activities fit in the pattern, but not in the location. Libby's wolf and door scratches, for instance." Jimmy moved his finger across the map. "If I looked at this pattern purely in terms of criminal activity, say a home robber or the like, I'd probably conclude the perpetrator began his career right here, in this inner ring of dots, and gradually moved outward as his confidence grew."

"What about those dots way out of the pattern?"

Jimmy scratched his chin. "Some could mean nothing. We might guess the others are personal, someone who crossed the witch maybe, or threatened him or her in some way. That's if it is a witch."

"Like Amå. She crossed the witch."

Jimmy nodded. "Or like Libby."

Eagle Feather regarded Jimmy. "How could Libby have crossed a witch? She hardly leaves the house."

"Maybe it wasn't Libby. Maybe it was Zack...or you."

Eagle Feather leaned back in his chair, eyes on Jimmy. "You could be right. We need to go over our back trails."

"I need to look back at every complaint, see how they fit the pattern. I plan to ask around out there, see if people have suspicions, or if anyone is pointing fingers." He glanced at Eagle Feather. "You could talk to Zack about what he's been up to lately. Why did this witch target his house?"

The men left the station at the same time. Jimmy drove north to Moenave, Eagle Feather west to Tuba City and Zack's office.

The road to Moenave was dirt, a straight line in the middle of nowhere. Jimmy pushed the Blazer along the barren flatland at a constant fifty, kicking up a large cloud of dust. The road was an arrow pointed northwest at distant bluffs until a sharp turn and a swing north aimed him toward another set of cliffs, much closer, soaring high up above the plateau. The road ended at an intersection just before them. Jimmy slid to a stop, his dust catching up to the truck. A right turn would take him along Reservation Road 1011 toward the Valley of Springs, the left to Moenave. He turned left.

Moenave was tucked in a wide break in the cliffs where water had etched out a valley over the eons. There were several springs on the mesa top, springs that gave life to the arid land below. The outflow stream coursed along rectangular side-by-side fields, its water long since sucked away for irrigation. Homes were scattered about, some near the fields, others out in the flatlands beyond the protection of the cliffs.

There was no town center, only a cluster of homes just off the roadway. Jimmy was familiar with the area, had been called out here on many occasions. He drove to one of the buildings that served as a general store, providing necessities to those who had neither the time nor wherewithal to drive all the way to Tuba City. Known locally as Slack Jack's, the small store exterior gave no indication of its purpose, other than a solitary advertisement for chewing tobacco.

Jimmy slid the Blazer to a stop, climbed out. He pushed the blanket in the doorway aside and stepped into the dim interior. Several men sat on benches, drinking beer and chewing the fat. One of them, a large man close to 300 pounds was Slack Jack himself. He stared at Jimmy when he entered. The conversation trailed off, all heads turned to the intruder.

"*Yá'át'ééh,*" Jimmy said.

Jack raised a hand of greeting from his copious lap.

"Anything in the pot, Jack?"

Jack waved a beefy arm toward a table. Jimmy walked over, found a cup less stained than most, blew in it and poured in the black liquid. He dumped in some sugar, disdaining the yellow solidified milk in a pitcher.

He turned, waited. Jack made the sign for sit-stay. Jimmy sat. An old man, his face weathered and wrinkled, regarded him. "*Yá'át'ééh,* Jimmy. We don't see you here so much these days. Too busy in the big city?"

Jimmy grinned. "Maybe I don't come here so much, but I talk to people here more than most other places." He pantomimed a phone to his ear with his hand.

The men looked puzzled, chewed on Jimmy's words for a while.

"I get more complaint calls from out here than anywhere else," Jimmy said, finally.

CAT

A beefy man with a large thunderbird tattoo on his arm stared at Jimmy. "Many people have lost animals. The police do nothing."

Jimmy looked at him, looked at the others, waited.

"Just last night my *ádí* Lori Welkai saw a *chindi* near Willow Creek," said another man, one they called Yellow Teeth.

Thunderbird tattoo spoke again. "I ask you this— what animal kills but does not eat the flesh? You cops tell me a coyote killed all those sheep, but a coyote kills to eat. You say a wolf killed the goats, but a wolf kills to eat. Does a wolf or coyote bang on hogan walls, knock at windows, scrape at the roof? All of this has happened. Where are the police? What causes this if not a *ánt'įįhnii?*"

"A skinwalker is that what you think?"

The men stared at Jimmy. No one answered.

"Nothing has been proven. Where are the police? I am here. If you think there is a skinwalker in Moenave, give me evidence, give me a lead I can follow."

Silence followed his words. He waited, keeping his eyes on the floor.

Jack spoke in a hushed voice. "Everyone knows the skinwalker will come for the one who betrays him."

"How could he know who? Is he here now? Is he one of you?"

There were loud denials.

"No one can know what names are spoken here, unless one of us tells someone else." Jimmy stood, took another sip of his coffee, put the cup back on the table.

"Thank you for the coffee."

He walked to the door, paused, looked back.

"When things like this happen, someone always knows where it comes from. Someone knows. If a name were to come to me in a note, how could I know who sent it?"

Jimmy regarded the silent men, pushed the blanket aside, stepped out into the bright sun.

CHAPTER TWENTY-ONE

Libby was hurt and angry. Zack didn't bother to answer his phone when she needed him most. He said his cell had no service, but she suspected he had it turned off. She shouldn't have to call Eagle Feather or Jimmy for help when Zack was around. And to think he drove right past here after he'd been away all night hunting a dangerous mountain lion and didn't even call. To Libby, it was evidence she was not a priority in Zack's mind. Any one of his friends and colleagues came first, it seemed.

Libby had risen early, before Zack was awake. She was still smoldering. She scooped up Bernie, blankets and all, carried him with her to the barn. She half hoped Zack would come find her, try to smooth things over, but when she heard the truck start up, wheels crunch gravel, it was clear that wasn't going to happen. Her anger grew all over again. How could he leave her and Bernie unprotected after what happened last night? Furious, she returned with Bernie to the house. She woke her sleeping boy, fed them both, and started in on the dishes, trying to calm down. She was still simmering when the doorbell rang.

Libby was surprised to see the old Navajo on her doorstep, wide brimmed reservation hat in his hands, kindly eyes cast downward. She recognized him. She'd seen him a number of times around the Trading Post and in the Navajo Interactive Museum in Tuba City where he volunteered his services guiding people through the exhibits. Libby knew he had a wealth of knowledge about Navajo culture. Word was he had managed to avoid the *belagaana* assimilation program, the forced re-education of Navajo children at special boarding schools. Instead, he learned at his father's knee, learned the old traditions of the Diné. Here he was on her porch, sweaty and dusty.

The old man saw the surprise on Libby's face. He smiled, nodded. "*Yá'át'ééh. Shí éí Naatnish yinishyé.* I am from the Navajo Museum. I have come to raise funds. Important funding was taken away, people fear the Museum will close." The ancient Navajo waved an arm to indicate the neighborhood. "I have come to the ranches and homes of wealthy people. They have been generous."

Libby laughed. "No wealthy person lives here." She glanced at the empty drive. "How did you come? You didn't walk this whole way, did you?"

The old man smiled, shook his head. "They gave me a ride to the road turnoff, I only walked from there."

"You poor man, that is still several miles. You must be thirsty. Here, come in." Libby stepped back, opened the door wide. "Let me offer you something to drink and a chance to rest. We can speak of donations then." She led the way to the kitchen.

"*Ahéhee*". The ancient one shuffled into the house behind Libby. He stood until Libby indicated the bench at the table.

"Is iced tea okay? Naatnish? You said that was your name?"

CAT

The old man turned thoughtful eyes to Libby, nodded. "You understand Navajo?"

"Oh, no, not at all. I've lived here all my life, some of it had to rub off."

"I am called Nate."

"Okay, Nate. Sugar?"

Nate smiled. "Plenty."

Libby set the glass on the table, the sugar bowl next to it.

Nate peered at Libby. "I have seen you at the Museum."

"I also remember you. I have visited the Trading Post since I was a child."

Nate nodded, his face showed approval. "It is good to understand the culture of a people who are your neighbors. Some Whites do not take the time." He added a large scoop of sugar to his tea, picked up the glass and sipped.

Libby smiled. "I'll go write a check for you. I'll just be a minute."

Nate looked up. "May I use your bathroom?"

"Of course. It's right through there."

When Libby returned with a check in hand, the old man was back in the kitchen. He was by the sink, his gaze out the window at the meadow and the hills.

"You live in a beautiful place. You are not lonely?"

"I'm seldom lonely. I have my child, and, of course, my husband"

Nate turned to look at her. "He is not here."

Libby felt some discomfort at the direction of the conversation. "You must know my husband—he is the FBI Supervisory Agent for the area. His office is not so far from the museum."

The old Indian gazed at her. "He is called away often?"

Libby felt more discomfort. "Not that often," she lied. "In fact, he was in Tuba City this morning. He could be home at any time."

A gentle smile creased Nate's face. "Yes, of course." He took the check from Libby, turned and walked through the living room to the front door. Libby followed.

At the door, Nate turned to her, his eyes crinkled with humor. "Where is your son?"

"He is napping. He will be up soon." Why so many questions, she wondered.

"It is good to rest." Nate stepped to the porch. "You have been kind." Another gentle look came from kindly eyes. "*Ahéhee*". He turned away.

Libby watched him negotiate the steps one at a time, his slow unsteady walk down the drive—a very old man. There was no reason to feel anxious around him.

Yet when she closed the door, she took care to lock it.

CHAPTER TWENTY-TWO

With nothing else to go on, Jimmy Chaparral decided to check out Yellow Teeth's story and visit Lori Welkai. As it happened, she was an old friend of his mother. He'd never met her. He thought he knew where she lived, northwest by the cliffs along Willow Creek above Hamblin Wash. It was a long way, almost to Route 69, but on decent road. Jimmy pushed the Blazer speed until it shuddered in protest.

Just beyond the westward bend of Route 23, a trace road angled off. Jimmy saw it at the last minute, jammed on his brakes, and shifted the Blazer to four-wheel drive. This area was new to him. He'd heard there were a few private homes, for the most part traditional hogans nestled along Willow Creek. The people still survived by grazing sheep and raising a small crop. He'd heard Lori Welkai and her family lived in one of these. He hoped to see where she had seen the *chindi,* and what she thought it meant.

Jimmy suspected people here might take exception to his visit; there was a tendency in the less populous regions to shoot first, ask questions later. He remained alert as he drove.

The rough track took him toward a line of trees along the creek, then angled northeast parallel to it. Multicolored bluffs loomed on either side in sharp contrast to the green of the cottonwoods. The cliffs inched closer

as he progressed until they became a narrow notch far
ahead. Well before that, he came to a log hogan among the
trees by the creek, with a smaller building, barn and corral.
A pickup truck sat next to the hogan.

Jimmy turned into the drive, pulled up just short of
the house, stopped and waited. The door cracked open. He
took that as an invitation and idled the truck forward,
parked near the pickup. He stepped out and walked to the
house.

When he knocked on the partly open door, a
young boy came out of the shadows. The boy looked up at
him, all Navajo but for startling blue eyes.

"*Yá'át'ééh.* I am Lieutenant Chaparral of the Navajo
Nation Police. I wish to speak with your mother. Is she
here?"

The boy shook his head.

"Is there anyone else at home?"

"My *amá sání* is here."

"Your grandmother is here? May I see her?"

A low, husky voice called from another room. The
boy pushed the door wide. Jimmy followed him inside.
They were in a short hall, dark but for the light emitted
from a doorway beyond. The boy showed Jimmy into that
room.

An old woman sat in a rocker near the window, her
lap covered by a shawl of bright colors and dynamic
design. Her gray hair was streaked with black, bundled,
knotted, her features sun-darkened, her eyes twinkling.

"Jimmy Chaparral, please sit."

CAT

Jimmy's eyes widened with surprise.

Her laugh was a pleasant low rumble. "You don't remember me, but I knew your mother. We were schoolgirls together, long ago. I am Lori Welkai."

Jimmy put his hat on a table and sat in the chair next to it. "Boarding school?"

She smiled. Her hands worked at the weave of the shawl, as if to inspect it by feel, but her eyes were on Jimmy. "They sent us to St. Louis in a train. We were allowed to come home twice a year. Your *amá* must have told you all about it."

"She did. Many times."

"I was sorry to hear she was gone." Lori's look was gentle. "I don't suppose you came here to talk about your mother."

Jimmy shook his head. "I came to talk about the *chindi*. They told me you saw one near here."

"Why on earth would you be interested in such a thing? It is not good to see the *ch'įįdii*, or sense it nearby. Who told you about that?"

Jimmy explained the recent circumstances, how the man at Slack Jack's had mentioned her story.

"Ah, the *ánt'įįhnii*. You think maybe what I saw has to do with him?"

Jimmy's eyes widened. "You know about the skinwalker?"

She nodded. "I have listened to the talk. The signs are there."

"I wish to put a name to him, to stop him, to stop the fear," Jimmy said.

"That is what we all want. But to name him—it will be difficult." Her hands stopped their movement. She studied him. "It is not impossible."

Jimmy waited.

"Yellow Teeth was right to mention me. I believe the *chindi* is a sign of the presence of *yee naaldlooshii*. I believe it lives not far away, otherwise the *chindi* would not walk here. A *ch'įįdii* is never far from its earthly possessions or body. The skinwalker feeds on its malevolent spirit."

Jimmy watched her face. "This is a lonely place, not many houses. You must have some idea."

"It is not any of my neighbors on this side of the mountain. I have heard rumors of a place, some hogans built long ago at the headwaters of Willow Creek, at the springs. No roads go there."

"Have you been there?"

She shook her head. "From my childhood my parents warned of bad spirits beyond the pass up Willow Creek. We were told never to go there. Of course, it intrigued us. My brother and his friend snuck up that way, once. He told me they never reached the head of the creek; the way was too long, too difficult. He never said more about his adventure. I learned later they felt they were watched, grew nervous and turned back. His friend died in a car accident not too long after."

"And your brother?"

"He moved away from the reservation to go to college, later took a job in California. I do not see him very often."

"Have you known any others who have gone there?"

"No. People avoid the place."

"Can you show me where you saw the *chindi*?"

"Yes, I can show you." Lori summoned the boy. He appeared as if waiting for his cue. His grandmother leaned on his arm to rise from the chair.

Jimmy smiled at the boy. "What is your name?"

The boy looked away. Lori spoke for him. "His name is Jacob. His father was a Hamblin descendent, as you can see by his eyes."

"He doesn't speak?"

"He is very shy. I fear he does not see enough people." She patted Jacob's hand, slipped her arm away. The boy disappeared. Lori led Jimmy out of the hogan with a spryness he had not suspected.

"I do not encourage Jacob to learn about such things as *chirdi* or *yee naaldlooshii*. He will know these things soon enough. He lost both parents to alcohol and drug related accidents, one after the other. He has spoken very little since then, hardly ever to strangers."

She steered Jimmy toward the old truck. "We will need to drive, I no longer walk such distances." Lori opened the pickup door. Before Jimmy could assist, she climbed into the driver's seat. "I'm not crippled, young man, just a little unsteady on my feet these days."

Jimmy got in the passenger side. The engine sputtered, caught. Lori released the clutch, worked the long floor shift, and they lurched forward. The truck bounced across the field to the dirt track. They followed it north toward the notch. Jimmy saw other houses along the way, mostly hogans, all traditional in appearance, tucked in close to the creek.

Lori released a hand from the wheel, waved at the buildings. "More people lived here back in the day. The young people don't like it. They say it is too isolated and move away. Now the older ones are dying. Another ten years, no one will live here."

"How far does this road go?"

"Just to that break in the cliffs. There is a path after that, just a horse trail. We won't go that far." True to her word, they turned toward the creek on a set of tire tracks. They forded the stream, just a trickle here, and climbed the easy slope on the far side.

"Jacob and I come here sometimes with sandwiches. It is a quiet and beautiful place."

A copse of cottonwood trees formed a bower; the grass was tall and green around a cracked and rotted picnic table. Beyond the clearing, the arid land encroached, beyond that, the multi-hued cliffs rose precipitously.

Lori stopped the truck but made no move to get out, instead pointed toward the cliffs through the windshield. "Just there, if you look close, you can see an old trail on the cliff face. Do you see it?"

Jimmy stared. "No."

"See the clump of brush at the base? It starts just there."

Jimmy saw it now, a faint line angling steeply up the face of the bluff. "Got it."

"That's where I saw it, on that trail."

"Just standing there? Going up the trail?"

"It was an outline, a shadow, it moved as a man moves. It was climbing the trail. In direct sunlight it disappeared, but I could see it in the shadow, as if it had no flesh."

Jimmy glanced at Lori. "You think maybe there's someone buried up there? Someone whose *chindi* hangs around?"

"Why else would it be here?"

"Has anyone else seen it?"

"I do not know. If anyone did see it, they won't talk about it." Lori settled back in the truck seat. "Jacob was with me that day, there at the table. I saw it on the cliff face when the movement caught my eye. I knew right away what it was. Jacob may have seen it, I don't know. If he did, he never mentioned it."

Jimmy thought about it. "Maybe there are Anasazi ruins up there somewhere, or an old burial site. Could be the *chindi* hangs around there."

"Could be. There are many ruins in this area." Lori leaned forward, started the truck, put it in gear. "This is as far as I go."

CHAPTER TWENTY-THREE

"Raptor? You said the sample was from a raptor? Are you sure about that?" Zack stared at Linda.

"Yeah, a giant bird. You know—flap, flap."

Zack shook his head in disbelief. He took another look at the monitor.

Linda came, looked over his shoulder. "I think you got it right. A single hand compressed the throat with one rapid squeeze. And yes, I'll buy into your theory it's the right hand."

"Where do we go from here?"

"Maybe you should call the local ornithology club." Linda sniggered, stopped when Zack sent her a withering look. "Well, we know a bird didn't kill this woman, of course. We need to find out how that talon residue got there, and see if we can learn more about the killer. I'll try to extract some DNA from your swabs. But for anything else, I'll need to inspect the body. When do we get it?"

"We don't."

"We don't..." She stared at him. "Oh, yeah. Traditions, taboos and such."

Zack nodded.

"Well, that's gonna make things difficult."

"How long will the DNA testing take?"

"A couple of days if I send it to our Prescott lab, even longer if they decide its not human 'cause then they'll have to send it to a specialized lab to figure out what it is."

Zack felt a wave of discouragement. "So it might take up to a week."

"Yeah, if I send it to Prescott." Linda's mouth turned up in a slight smile. "But I'm gonna send it to Florida."

"What? Why so far? Why Florida?"

"The William R. Maples Center for Forensic Medicine is down there. It's at the University of Florida's College of Medicine. They specialize in the genetic analysis of companion animals and wildlife. There's a DNA analyst on staff specifically for animal casework. So if they decide its animal, they don't have to send it anywhere else, and we get it back that much sooner."

"Well, that's great."

"Just one problem."

"Ah, the other shoe."

"It will have to come out of your budget."

Zack didn't hesitate. "Go ahead. We've got to know who or what we're dealing with."

Linda began to label and package the samples for their trip. "You know what I think?" she said, as she typed a label.

Zack shook his head.

"I think whoever strangled this woman had an eagle claw gripped inside his thumb and index finger and he squeezed that around her neck. A real showman."

"I can only hope you're right."

A knock sounded on the lab door and it swung open. Eagle Feather peered in. "'Room for another?"

"Well, hail, hail the gang's all here," Linda said.

Zack waved his friend in.

The Navajo pulled out a stool next to Zack. "Who do you think killed Amå?"

"So you know about that already."

"Yes, I just came from Jimmy's office. He is worried people will panic if they think there is a skinwalker out there."

Zack shook his head in disgust. "That's just what we're trying to disprove as fast as we can."

"Can you?"

"Well, no—not yet. We have to wait for DNA tests."

"What have you got so far?"

Linda giggled. "Flap, flap."

Eagle Feather stared at her, looked at Zack. "What's the matter with her?"

Zack groaned. "So far our tissue samples point to a large bird as the killer."

Eagle Feather raised his eyebrows.

Zack pointed to the monitor on the wall. "Go take a close look."

Eagle Feather went to study the photo.

"While you're over there, bear this little fact in mind: Linda analyzed the residue I swabbed from each of those fingernail punctures. She found keratin specific to either a large lizard or a raptor."

Eagle Feather's head swung round, first to Zack, then Linda.

Linda smiled.

"This won't help Jimmy's cause," Eagle Feather said. He came back to his stool. "Speaking of that, Jimmy had an interesting thought. He's investigating this from the opposite angle, trying to make the case for a skinwalker as the killer. That way, if it turns out he can not prove it, people around here are more likely to accept the results, and things might quiet down."

"Smart. How's he going about it?" Zack asked.

"He has mapped out the locations of recent complaints, all the stock mutilations, strange sightings, missing pets, and similar incidents. The epicenter appears to be near Moenave. He went up there to talk to people, to see what is going on. He found a few anomalies, the right kind of reports, but way out of the pattern. From a skinwalker point of view, if we think that way, those could be personal attacks, like people who crossed him—Amá, for instance."

"Makes sense—if you think like a witch, that is."

"I thought so too." Eagle Feather spun his stool to face Zack. "One of those anomalies was Libby's wolf sighting and the clawing at your front door." The Navajo leaned toward Zack. "So I must ask you, White Man, what have you done lately to piss off a skinwalker?"

CHAPTER TWENTY-FOUR

Jimmy helped Lori up the steps to her house, as much as she would permit him, thanked her and said his goodbyes. Her final look warned him to be careful.

Back in the Blazer, he drove to the clearing. This time he went beyond the picnic bench, out of the trees onto the sand. With the truck in four-wheel drive, he wove among the sage and coyote brush until he reached the base of the cliffs.

The sun was hot outside the truck. He rummaged for his water bottle and sipped while he studied the cliff face. There was an atmosphere of agelessness to the place, enduring, untouched for a thousand years. The old trail angled above him. It originated somewhere to his left. As he walked that way each step stirred dust, left tracks where none had been before.

The trailhead had eroded into a heap of crumbled sandstone. Jimmy climbed gingerly until the trail became more evident, foot-hardened. It ascended along a natural fault line, widened by human hands, maybe even stone tools, Jimmy thought, eyeing marks on the inside wall. The path surface was undisturbed. He might well be the first to ascend this path since the Old Ones.

A short climb brought him above tree level. With each step, his view of the picnic grove, and the entire Willow Creek Valley improved. It was spectacular. The Echo Cliffs towered over the wide expanse of the Hamblin

Wash. Although steep, the trail was well contoured and relatively easy to climb. Jimmy saw no evidence anyone had passed here since it was first built.

At the top of the bluff, Jimmy paused to become oriented. The pathway disappeared on the stone surface of the mesa top Ahead, to the north, he could now see a large arroyo slashed into the cliffs, beyond which the bluffs marched up to the notch carved by Willow Creek.

The arroyo was hidden from anyone in the valley below, where the cliff face must appear seamless. Jimmy doubted anyone suspected its presence.

Stones marked the way across the tableland. As he came near, the opposite wall of the arroyo came into better view. The precipitous face was smooth, painted with streaks of desert varnish. Several yards below, horizontal layers interrupted the surface where sandstone protruded, like an unevenly stacked deck of cards. Within the crooked jumbled ledges a straight line caught his eye, too perfect for nature. It was a wall of earthen bricks, he realized, stacked across a crevice between layers. It must be an Anasazi granary.

The discovery was no surprise. The *chindi* Lori saw had to be linked to a grave or spiritual center somewhere. It would not travel far from it. Jimmy was sure there was a cliff dwelling somewhere in that craggy face above the arroyo headwall. If undisturbed, the bones of the Anasazi people might still lie there.

Was there a relationship between the *chindi* Lori had seen and the suspected skinwalker they sought? Or was it coincidence? You could have a *chindi* without the skinwalker, but it was unlikely to have the skinwalker without a *chindi*. If Lori's suspicions were correct, and a witch lived at the headwaters of Willow Creek, there could be a connection. If so, he planned to find evidence of it.

The ancient path across the barren sandstone topland passed a row of rocks, little stones piled one on the other, a sort of rectangular barrier around a flat area. The Anasazi might have grown corn here and stored the maize in the granary he'd seen. A cliff dwelling would be in the arroyo, not on the mesa top, but the trail should lead him to it. The sun pounded down, merciless even this late in the season, reflecting off the sand beneath his feet. He dripped sweat.

The trail brought him to the arroyo headwall, ended at an opening in the sandstone at his feet. Through it Jimmy saw a large hollow widened by ancient floods. A vertical wall fell away, parts of an old ladder fashioned from logs and sinew lay crumpled on the cave floor. It had once stood against the wall for easier access.

It must be ten or twelve feet to the bottom, not so far, Jimmy thought. There were some protrusions for hand and foot holds. He didn't allow himself time to consider but went for it, half down climbing, half falling. In minutes he stood on the slick sandstone surface within the hollow. It was in effect a natural bridge formed by erosion from floodwaters rushing into the arroyo, burrowing a hole in the sandstone cliff, and widening it over the centuries. Opposite was another vertical wall to the surface. Ahead the floor sloped and dropped away out of sight over the cliff face, like the top of a waterslide. The entire hollow glowed with a translucent effect from the lowering sun. Two black handprints on the sidewall appeared near the head of the drop off. To Jimmy, they confirmed an entranceway.

The floor surface was glassy. Jimmy inched along it, expecting the cliff dwelling to reveal itself in some way.

The Navajo were inclined to avoid an Anasazi ruin under most circumstances. Lieutenant Chaparral was one hundred percent Navajo, despite his police training and exposure to the white man's world. Anasazi is Navajo for "Ancient Enemy"; evil lurked in these places and should not to be disturbed. Jimmy had no doubt the *chindi* Lori had seen came from here.

There was no way forward other than the slick slide, no way to know what lay beyond it. At worst, it was a device to launch enemies over the cliff edge to their doom. At best, it could propel him directly into an Anasazi ruin, a prospect that did not excite him either. The slide might well be the only egress, a defensive device. There probably had been a system of ladders, long since decayed.

Unwilling to risk his life, Jimmy edged back from the slide and crawled to the place he had entered. The climb to the surface appeared higher now, the handholds fewer. Jimmy began to climb, but slipped. He tried again; gained a few feet, fell off again. He studied the wall, searched for a route.

A percussive sound, deep, booming, like a bass drum in some vast room came from somewhere below. Before the echo faded, another sounded.

Someone, something was down there..

CHAPTER TWENTY-FIVE

Zack and Eagle Feather walked out of the FBI building together, Zack to go home, Eagle Feather to head to the Grand Canyon to check for more recent cat sign. They drove away in tandem; the old red truck followed Zack's Jeep CJ.

Zack knew he had some backfilling to do with Libby, after which he needed to talk through the skinwalker thing with her. Eagle Feather's words hung in his ears. He couldn't imagine Libby doing anything to aggravate some delusional shaman, but one never knew.

Zack was used to threats. His job meant having enemies. This was different, personal. Someone seemed to be trying to reach him through his wife. At first he thought it was because of his visit with Amå, meant as a warning, but the timing didn't work. The attack on his house and the visit with Amå overlapped, many miles apart.

Zack glanced at the red truck in his mirror. He wondered about Eagle Feather. He knew his friend, saw through that opaque exterior to an unusual inner tension. The man was obsessed with this mountain lion—fighting guilt, probably. Zack was worried about him.

They parted ways at the ranch turnoff; the red truck roared past with a honk. Zack took his time on the drive to the house thinking out his approach. He decided a diversion might work best.

He found Libby in the kitchen, her back to him, drying a glass. She'd heard the door open, knew he was there. He saw the rigid set of her shoulders, the tension in her slender body.

"I'm very worried about Eagle Feather."

"You ought to be worried about yourself." She didn't turn.

"I'm worried Eagle Feather might harm himself."

She turned part way now, glanced at him. "Why on earth would Eagle Feather harm himself?"

Zack sat on the edge of the bench. The room smelled of dish soap and bacon, a homey scent he loved. "He's taking the lion incident personally. He's heaped guilt on himself."

"Eagle Feather would never harm himself, it's not in his nature."

"It's in his nature to throw himself into the pursuit of this lion so intently he takes needless risks."

Libby turned back to the sink. "Maybe you should go with your friend if he needs you."

Zack sighed. "He won't listen to me any more than you do when I say I'm sorry. You are both very stubborn."

Libby spun around, the dishtowel in her hand. "Don't you compare me to your friends, Zachary Tolliver. You don't drop everything and come running when *I* need you, as you do Eagle Feather." Her dark eyes glistened with anger.

"If I knew you needed me, I would have. I didn't see it, I am sorry."

"Zack, you know less about what happens here than what happens on the entire Reservation. I can never reach you, and you never call. What if that old Navajo who came here today had meant me harm?"

Zack's head came up. "What old Navajo?"

Libby leaned back against the counter. "That old man from the museum, Naatnish. He was going house-to-house collecting money for a fund drive. He's harmless, but what if he wasn't? Bernie and I are isolated out here. We need to be able to reach you."

"Did you let him in?"

"Of course. I couldn't leave him on the doorstep. I gave him some water and wrote a check."

Zack had it in mind to reprimand her for such a risk, but thought better of it. He took out his phone. "You're right. It is isolated here. We've always known it, but we trust our neighbors." He found a number, punched it in. "We had more neighbors in the past. Now the young people have grown, they've moved away, allowed the Reservation to absorb their properties. Now our nearest neighbor is a half-mile away." Zack heard a voice answer his ring.

"Navajo Interactive Museum."

"Hi, George, this is Zack Tolliver calling. I just called to ask how the fund drive is going, and if we can help in any way."

"What fund drive is that?"

"Well, Naatnish dropped by here earlier to pick up a check for a fund drive for the museum."

"Uh, just a minute, Zack." Zack heard the muffling of a hand over the phone and some low voices.

George was back. "Zack, there must be some mistake. We don't have a fund drive going right now. This is very strange. I guess the old man must be confused. You should cancel that check. We'll return it when he brings it in."

Zack signed off, looked at Libby. "I think we just proved your point."

Libby put her hand over her mouth, stared back at Zack.

CHAPTER TWENTY-SIX

For the first time that day, Jimmy remembered the rifle he'd left back in the Blazer. That was stupid. He should've brought it, despite the extra weight. Customarily, he would be armed with a handgun, but that too was in the Blazer, belt and holster behind the seat, all surrendered in the name of comfort. Stupid.

Jimmy remembered his old instructor's axiom, "You will need your weapons most when you think you need them least". He had two choices now: climb the wall, or commit himself to the slide and take his chances. To his mind, the second choice was not a real option.

He stood back, studied the sandstone face before him. He was athletic and agile, but no climber. The handholds looked larger than they felt once he tried to grip them. There had been no sound from below since the two booming noises. It could have been rocks falling, dislodged by erosion or by some cave dwelling animal.

As if in answer to his thoughts, another hollow boom sounded, louder than the first two. It was percussive, measured. This was no falling rock—it was deliberate. Somebody made that sound.

If someone with hostile intent came up from below, Jimmy was in an indefensible position, nowhere to run, no weapon. He glanced wildly around the hollow, remembered the opposite wall and went to it. It was the same height. He studied the nooks and nodules on it. There might be a way.

He reached high up the wall, found something to hold with his fingers, now worked his right foot up until he could weight it on something. It held while he explored with his left foot, found an edge, weighted that as well. It, too, held. Now he could free his left hand to reach higher. Groping, cheek against the cool stone, he felt his way up, hold by hold. He was actually climbing.

Unable to look up or down, his face pressed tight to the wall, Jimmy tried not to think about what might be below him, his mind completely focused on the act of climbing. When he felt the heat of the sun on the back of his reaching hand he knew he was close. Another short scramble, a difficult chin-up, a push-up and a slither, and Jimmy crawled onto the hot sandstone. He lay prostrate, relieved, catching his breath.

He was on the opposite wall from where he had climbed down. After a moment, he rolled to a sitting position, wiped the grit from his cheek, and looked across the void into the liquid yellow eyes of a huge mountain lion.

The animal crouched just across the cave opening, ten feet away. It was a monster, the largest cat Jimmy had ever seen. Its tail was thick as hawser rope, the tip of it twitched angrily. The cat's eyes radiated inexorable intent. Jimmy was captivated, fascinated by the immutable evil lurking within them. He was prey and he knew it—a rabbit caught too far from its hole. The great lion would be on him before he could move a muscle. It pinned him there with its eyes like a butterfly to a board.

When it leapt, the movement was imperceptible, faster than eye or brain could follow. It flew at him, over him, beyond him. Jimmy swung his head to follow, too late. It was gone, instantly melding into the terrain.

Jimmy gasped. A tremor gripped his limbs, his heart pounded against his chest wall like a caged thing. He felt too weak to move. Had the cat come from the ruin, had it somehow made those booming sounds? Why hadn't it attacked him? Where had it gone? His brain boiled over with questions.

One thing he knew for sure—this was no normal mountain lion. He'd seen many over his lifetime—in zoos, running wild, on trophy walls. None were so large, so mesmerizing, so...*human*.

He stood, shaking, then turned, walked to where he could cross over the arroyo. Fearful, he looked back over his shoulder. Something caught his eye. He turned, looked. A man stood on a distant ridge, a shadowy figure in a wide brimmed hat silhouetted against the fading blue sky—watching him.

CHAPTER TWENTY-SEVEN

Jimmy Chaparral glanced over his shoulder many times on the downward trail. The low angled sun was in his eyes each time he did and every clump of sage took on the aura of a mountain lion.

The moment he reached the Blazer, he retrieved his holster belt from behind the seat and strapped it on. Next came the rifle from the rack. The load checked, he laid it across the passenger seat within easy reach.

It was dusk by now, would be dark before long. Jimmy first drove to Lori's house. He warned her about the lion. "You'll want to keep your animals close."

She cocked an eyebrow at him. "Is that all I should worry about?"

He had started toward his truck, turned back. "Keep your doors and windows locked, too."

Just before he turned onto the pavement, Jimmy called stopped to Eagle Feather. The phone rang on and on, never went to a service. The man wasn't much for messages. He called Zack's home instead.

Libby answered. After a limited exchange, she put Zack on the line. Her voice sounded strained to Jimmy.

Zack sounded grim as well. "What's up, Jimmy?"

"Hey, Zack. I tried to reach Eagle Feather but he doesn't answer his phone. Any idea where he is?"

"He's at the South Rim, guarding the mules in case the lion comes back. He'll likely have his phone off."

"Umm..." Jimmy thought about how to handle this.

"Why, what's the matter, Jimmy?"

"I know where that mountain lion is and it's not up at the canyon. I also have a pretty good idea where we can find the guy who's digging up graveyards."

"You've had a busy day."

"You could say so. I went to Moenave and on to Willow Creek Canyon to see Lori Welkai. We should talk. How about a meeting—you, me, and Eagle Feather."

"Tomorrow?"

"Sooner the better. Can you do tomorrow morning at ten at the Wagon Wheel Trading Post in Cameron? We can meet at the food bar."

"I'll be there." Zack paused. "Jimmy, I need a favor. Can you send a man over to be with Libby and Bernie tomorrow? "

"Why? Something happen?" Jimmy switched his phone to the other ear.

"Libby had a visit today from Naatnish, the old guy at the Navajo Interpretive Museum. He lied about his reason for the visit. When you add to that someone carving up my front door, it gets worrisome. I won't leave her unless she's covered."

Jimmy agreed. He called and made the arrangements, put the truck in gear, turned right and headed west to Route 69. By the time he reached the turn-off for Tuba City, it was full dark.

☐~ ~ ~ ~ ~

It was 9:30 precisely when Jimmy turned into the parking lot of the Wagon Wheel the next morning. He'd seen a few flakes of snow as he drove down. The thin milky cloud layer had dirty patches on the underside. Winter wasn't far off.

He parked himself on a stool in the little restaurant, ordered black coffee. Sleep came slow last night; when it finally did it brought images of crouched mountain lions and hypnotic evil eyes.

The meeting time came and went. Jimmy ordered eggs. It was half an hour before Zack and Eagle Feather dropped onto stools on either side of him.

Zack apologized. "I waited for Eagle Feather to come by the house."

Eagle Feather wore a sheepish grin. "I had my phone off last night; didn't pick up my messages until this morning. Guess I must have dozed off for a while there."

The men ordered coffee.

"Zack tells me you've seen my mountain lion."

"I have."

Eagle Feather's eyes narrowed. "How do you know it's the same one?"

"It fits your description, the largest cat I've ever seen. There's something very different about that animal."

"Tell us," Zack said.

Jimmy told the whole story, about his stop at Slack Jack's, Yellow Tooth's comments, his subsequent visit with

CAT

Lori, his trek up to the Anasazi site, the meeting with the cat and the silhouette of the man on the ridge.

Jimmy's account was interrupted just once when the girl took their breakfast orders. He had his friends' rapt attention.

When the story ended, the questions began.

"So you never actually saw the Anasazi ruin?" Zack asked.

"I couldn't find a way down to it without risking my ass."

"You say the mountain lion jumped right over you?" Eagle Feather looked incredulous. "It didn't touch you?"

"It was over me before I even saw it move. By the time my head turned, it was gone."

"And right after that is when you saw the man on the far ridge?" Zack asked.

Jimmy nodded.

The waitress arrived with steaming dishes. The men ate, the only sound the clinking of utensils on plates.

Zack put down his fork. "Do you guys know Naatnish, the old guy who volunteers at the museum?"

"Sure." Jimmy said.

Eagle Feather nodded.

"What do you know about him?"

"Nice old guy, knows more than most about our culture," Jimmy said.

"Do you know where he lives?"

"Never thought about it."

"He's pretty much under everybody's radar, isn't he," Zack said.

Eagle Feather glanced at Zack. "What's going on with him?"

Zack shrugged. "Not sure. He showed up at my place soliciting funds for the museum. Libby was home all alone." "Unusual, not illegal," Jimmy said.

"Except he lied about the fund drive."

Both men turned to look at him.

"I checked with the museum. No fund drive. That's the reason I asked you to send a man to watch my house today."

"Why do you think Naatnish came to your house, then?" Jimmy asked.

"That's the big question, all right."

"A witch uses someone's personal belongings, like a sock or glove to place a curse," Jimmy said. "He wraps it around a potshard, like one you might find in an Anasazi ruin, for instance, and puts it in a tarantula hole."

Zack stared at him. "Thanks for that."

Eagle Feather caught his eye. "You might want to take this seriously. It may not seem like much, but add it to the visitor who scratched up your door, and that rattlesnake dropping on you, well—"

Jimmy nodded. "Eagle Feather's right. The point is the intent. Whether or not Naatnish is a witch or a skinwalker, whether or not you believe in all this, someone means you harm."

"Put it all together." Eagle Feather ticked them off on his fingers. "There's that uncharacteristic mountain lion attack that almost killed Prónto, then the snake, Amå's murder, the child's grave dug up, the *chindi* Lori sees, Jimmy's encounter with a huge mountain lion. Now you tell us about a strange visit from Naatnish. If someone is pretending to be a skinwalker, he's doing a very good job."

Zack shook his head. "You're throwing a lot of apples and oranges together. We have nothing to connect all those events."

"There speaks the White FBI Man who doesn't believe in coincidence."

Zack gave Eagle Feather an annoyed look. "Okay, look at it this way. How do you think it would appear if I filed a report to my superiors citing all those incidents? From a law enforcement point of view, an unknown assailant strangled a woman in her bed. That's it."

"An assailant that apparently was a large bird," Jimmy said, grinning.

"The jury's out on that one."

Eagle Feather threw up his hands. "I think we know we have a problem. Each of us should handle it as we normally would. Zack can work on it strictly as a murder case and see where that takes him. Jimmy can do the same as a Navajo Nation policeman, responsive to the cultural concerns of his people. I am the one with freedom to pursue this case as if the suspect is a skinwalker."

Zack nodded. "I like that. None of us need put ourselves in a position we can't support."

Jimmy's glance went from one man to the other. "That's all good, but we've got to keep this a team effort. We're gonna need each another before this thing is over."

Eagle Feather stood, slapped Jimmy on the back. "Do not worry, if we need to blame someone for our screw-ups, you are our man."

Jimmy dropped some bills on the counter. "My first inquiry will be about Naatnish and his irregular fund raising."

"I'm going to check with Linda, see what we've got on Amå's murder," Zack said. He glanced at Eagle Feather. "What's your plan?"

Eagle Feather reached down for his coffee cup, took a final sip, and grinned. "I have a mountain lion to hunt."

CHAPTER TWENTY-EIGHT

When Eagle Feather left the Trading Post parking lot he drove directly to his trailer. Jimmy's story confirmed in his mind what he already knew; this was no ordinary mountain lion. This hunt should not be taken lightly.

Immersed in Navajo traditions since childhood, Eagle Feather respected the potential power of Witchery Way. His college education balanced those cultural influences with an understanding of the physical world as interpreted by the human brain. He understood the tremendous power of suggestion, how it could determine his fear, his fight or flight response, no matter the amount of logic applied.

He decided to fight fire with fire.

He went to the barn, took a box of rifle cartridges from the back edge of the workbench and pocketed three. No ordinary bullets, these were tipped with white ash and were blessed by a shaman in a special ceremony. They were his aces in the hole.

Scudding black-bottomed clouds sailed a deep blue sky, a strong westerly wind bit cold on the back of his hands. In the tiny trailer kitchen he put together a couple of sandwiches, topped off his water bottle, and loaded his daypack.

Within the hour Eagle Feather approached the turnoff for Willow Creek Canyon. As his truck bounded in and out of chuckholes, he put a plan together. To his mind it would be futile to retrace Jimmy's steps up the ancient's trail to the Anasazi ruin. Skinwalker or real cat, the lion had long since gone.

Jimmy said the cat vanished to the north; the mysterious figure on the ridge was off in the same direction. The terrain to the north funneled into a narrow notch gouged out by Willow Creek on its southward journey. Eagle Feather thought the animal would in natural course pass through this gorge, likely ranging on up toward the creek headwaters. He'd heard rumors of someone who lived up there in a hand-built log hogan. The rumors said he was a witch, said he flew in and out at will.

To some people, anyone who lived a solitary life must be a witch. Eagle Feather guessed people likely thought he was a witch, too.

He drove past several hogans strung along the creek. One of them must be Lori Welkai's home. He stayed on the road which degraded to single tracks near the canyon narrows, eventually became a mere trace through the tall grass until it ended at a large mound of boulders.

He climbed out of the truck, stretched. The occasional sun bursts between cloud shadows felt hot, but the wind still blew cold. He was glad of his insulated vest and gloves.

Eagle Feather organized his gear. Rifle cartridges for the 30-30 went into the large vest pocket, the ash-dipped bullets into a trouser pocket. His pack with the sandwiches and water, a slicker, rappel gear, and a handgun went on his back. Before setting out, Eagle Feather paused to enjoy the vista of green cottonwoods below towering red cliffs framed by the blue cloud-mottled sky. In his opinion, this was the best argument against city living.

The passage through the creek narrows proved difficult, with no semblance of a path. It meant a vigorous scramble over boulders heaped along the creek, frothing below him down its steep rocky bed.

Beyond, once through the notch, the terrain softened, the creek spread wide and sandy, even disappeared in places. Mule deer, brown eyes wide, gazed at him, then bounded off as he came close. Here the land was parched and dry—sandy, dusty, streaked with gravel—a giant watershed where infrequent flash floods dropped their load of debris.

The ground left records of every animal that had passed here: raccoon, deer, feral pigs, and coyotes, even a bobcat. He found no mountain lion prints.

Further upstream, cottonwoods clustered in occasional dense copses. Sometimes the undergrowth, matted with driftwood, was too heavy to manage. Eagle Feather hiked wide around those places.

He paused for water. The sand in this valley was deep in places, almost like beach sand. It made for arduous trekking. Ahead, beyond the open watershed, the cliffs came together again to form another notch. Eagle Feather thought he saw a hint of green beyond; it might be the creek headwater.

He found the mountain lion tracks just a few yards from his rest spot. To Eagle Feather's mind, the same lion he followed into the Grand Canyon made them. The pad marks were fully six inches in diameter, the four pod marks clear in the soft sand. The prints were recent, might easily have been made yesterday or even last night after the cat's encounter with Jimmy Chaparral at the Anasazi ruin. The lion had angled across Eagle Feather's path, headed in the same general direction.

He followed. The prints took him toward the cliffs on the east side of the gap, and through it. They stayed high, just under the sheerest part of the cliff, across several boulder fields. Another spectacular view unfolded before him, a wide park created by two intersecting canyons. A ribbon of green marked the creek, wide in places, then narrow like an anaconda after its meal. The pancake flat desert valley was streaked with hues of tan, russet, bronze, and black. Bluffs of red, yellow, and orange surrounded it all. Cloud shadows, like dark secrets, glided across the valley floor.

Eagle Feather followed the mountain lion prints down into the basin, toward the ribbon of green foliage. Nearer the trees, he saw a small building, a traditional hogan. The lion tracks led directly to it.

Fifty yards from the building, the tracks disappeared. Beyond them, he found human footprints.

CHAPTER TWENTY-NINE

The Navajo Interpretive Museum, with its ribbed roof, suggested an oversized tent. Jimmy walked up the ramp and under the rainbow arch, dropped a few bills in the donation container. In the main exhibit space, he glanced toward each of the symbolic four corners, hoping to see Naatnish, but did not.

He walked to a side corridor, knocked on a door marked Staff Only and pushed it open in the same motion. George Bookbinder sat at a desk littered with folders, papers, and letters. He looked up, saw Jimmy, and smiled.

"*Yá'át'ééh*, Jimmy. We haven't seen you around here in a while."

Jimmy closed the door. "I should come by more often, if only to remind myself of my heritage from time to time. It is too easy to forget when you work with the *belagaana* every day."

"Is that why you've come today?"

Jimmy shook his head. "No. I came today to speak to Naatnish. Is he in?"

George stood, swept some brochures a folding chair. "Here, sit. Would you like some tea?"

Even before Jimmy nodded, George put a teabag in a cup and was pouring hot water over it from a plugin teapot. "Sugar? We don't have milk."

Jimmy shook his head, waved it away, took the cup from George, and sipped. "Good," he declared. After a polite moment he caught George's eye. "Naatnish?"

George leaned back in his chair. "I haven't seen Nate yet this morning. He volunteers, you know. Sort of keeps his own hours. He'll be here for a few days, absent the next three." George gave a rueful smile. "He got himself in a little hot water the other day, might be embarrassed to come in."

"Oh?"

"Old Nate, he's getting up there, you know. Sweet, sweet guy, but he gets confused easily these days. Took it upon himself to do a fund drive we hadn't authorized, went around to outlying ranchers." George lifted his eyebrows and grinned. "He did pretty darn well. We couldn't keep the money, of course."

"How many ranches did he visit?"

"We don't know, actually, but he had checks from several people. We're gonna return 'em."

Jimmy took another sip of tea. "Where does Nate live? I don't think I ever knew."

"I don't actually know, either. Because he's a volunteer, we don't require that kind of information—we don't need to write payroll checks or any reports. I always had the impression he lived out toward Moenkopi, or somewhere near there."

"How does he get here? Doesn't drive, does he?"

"Nah. He usually gets a ride from someone, or walks, I guess." George turned to face Jimmy square on. "Why this interest in Nate?"

Jimmy shrugged. "No big deal. I happened to talk to Zack Tolliver. He mentioned the old boy had been out to their place collecting funds. I told him I'd check on it."

George looked worried. "Zack's not gonna push this thing, is he? I mean Nate's an old guy, kinda addled. He didn't mean anything, I'm sure. He came in here all proud and handed over the pile of checks. Sure didn't plan to keep 'em."

"No, no. Zack was just concerned for the guy's safety. I mean, how'd he get all the way our there without a vehicle? Hitchin' is all right around here where everyone knows him. But out there, he might get stuck, nobody pick him up. Or worse, the wrong person pick him up, if you know what I mean."

George nodded in agreement. "I got no idea how he got out there and back. It is worrisome, particularly since I wonder if he actually knows where he is sometimes."

Jimmy handed George his business card. "This is the cell phone I'll be using. Call me if he comes in, okay?"

"Sure thing."

Outside, Jimmy called Danny Kykotsa on his cell. Danny lived in Lower Moenkopi but had spent many years as a Hopi Ranger. If he didn't know something about Naatnish, he d know someone who did. They agreed to meet at the Hopi Legacy Inn & Suites coffee bar.

R LAWSON GAMBLE

Jimmy climbed back into the Blazer and drove south out of town toward Moenkopi. Twenty minutes later, he strode across the shiny tiled floor with its Hopi Tribe logo and shook Danny's hand. They found a small table near the coffee bar. Jimmy let the man buy him a coffee, even though he'd had too much already.

Danny was short, thick and bronzed. His face always wore a smile. The two men, one Hopi, the other Navajo, were friends of several years. The Rangers were a Hopi vigilante group back in the day, now evolved into the officially recognized police force. Although Danny didn't stay on to make the transition, he was helpful to Jimmy when it was necessary to cross reservation lines, as now. Moenkopi is an exclave of the Hopi Reservation, completely surrounded by the larger Navajo Reservation. Jimmy knew the Hopi were sensitive about official intrusions by their neighbors.

"Yeah, I know who you mean, the old guy I always see at the museum in Tuba City. What makes you think he's got anything to do with us?" Danny's elbows rested on the table, his intense hazel eyes on Jimmy.

Jimmy shrugged. "I don't, really. No one seems to know where he comes from. The museum director, George Bookbinder, thought he lived out here somewhere. I had always assumed he was a Navajo, 'cause he sure loves that museum."

"It's not unheard of for a Navajo to live on the Hopi Rez, but not in the villages, unless they intermarry, which doesn't seem likely in this case. Still, some of the

Navajo have ancient roots up on the Moenkopi Plateau and other outlying areas that have since became the preserve of the Hopi. A few are still there."

"Like Emma Truewoman and her mom, for instance?"

Danny looked at Jimmy in surprise. "Emma's mom?"

"You know, Amå, as she calls her, the crystal gazer, lived in that old hogan on the mesa."

"The one who was killed? That old lady wasn't Emma's mom. Emma lives right here in Moenkopi."

Jimmy set his coffee down, sloshing it. "Not her mom? I've been out to that hogan many times. Emma is always there to meet me. She calls the old lady her mother, walks around there like she owns the place. I assumed they lived together."

Danny shook his head. "She likely called her Amå as a sign of respect, not specifically as her mother. Emma could be her student, I suppose. Or..."

"What?"

"It's rumored Amå has a lot of cash stashed somewhere up there. She supposedly benefits from a trust from some relative. Money comes in, but doesn't go out; she never spends any, so people figure she's hoarding it."

Jimmy stared at Danny. "You think Emma is..."

Danny raised both hands. "Don't want to wrong the woman. Just sayin', that's the rumor."

Jimmy shook his head, decided to mull it over later. "So you can't help me with Naatnish."

"Why not ask Emma herself? She's been around here longer than me, she may know." Danny grinned. "Sounds like you have a few other questions to ask her, anyway."

Jimmy nodded in agreement, moved as if to rise. Danny rested a hand on his arm. "Emma can be difficult. I've had several run-ins with her in the past, usually to do with neighbors and property and such. Blasted a hole in a neighbor's house with that shotgun one time. Just thought you should know when you go looking for her."

CHAPTER THIRTY

Linda absently took a bite of jelly donut, her eyes glued to her computer screen as Zack came in. Bits of sticky red filling clung to the surface of her mouse.

She looked up. There was powdered sugar on her lips. "You're just in time," she said. "I have a preliminary report from Florida."

"That was quick."

"It's another reason I like the Maples Center, they're fast." Linda's eyes stayed on the screen during the conversation. She scrolled with one hand, held the donut in the other. "Look at this. They found enough tissue cells to run a test, but they say the sample we sent is tainted. The fast and furious first run returned an impossibility." Linda pulled her eyes away from the screen to look at Zack.

"Well?"

Linda smirked. "They found two equal strands of DNA in the one sample; one was of an owl, the other a man."

Zack raised his eyebrows. "Meaning..."

"Nothing. Like I said, it's a preliminary run. They've rejected these results, they'll do another; a more thorough one."

Zack pulled out a stool, sat down. "Why'd they send it if they rejected it?"

Linda took another bite of the donut. She chewed and swallowed before she answered. "That's another thing I like about this lab; it's their policy to send all the data resulting from tests, regardless, so the client can see the process. Sometimes, it makes a difference."

Linda scrolled to the top of her screen. "Here, this is the letter from the technician." She read aloud. "Ms. Whittaker, the results of this preliminary DNA run are clearly erroneous. It is likely the sample you sent was tainted by an owl sample. We will complete the testing to be certain, but suggest you send a second sample if at all possible, etc., etc."

Linda grinned at Zack, her eyes teased. "How did they know the sample comes from a skinwalker in the form of an owl?"

Zack didn't smile. "Not a word of this to anyone, Linda. If this gets out, people around here will panic. They'll see it as scientific proof of their greatest nightmare."

"Does that include Jimmy?"

"Especially Jimmy. This is FBI classified material as of now. Wait for the full run."

Linda gave a mock salute with one hand, took the last bite of the jelly donut with the other.

Zack spun on the stool to face her. "Is the human DNA strand complete enough to draw conclusions if compared to a suspect?"

Linda nodded. "At least in a preliminary way. It would definitely be an indicator." She chuckled. "Find me the right owl, I'll identify that one also."

"Funny lady." Zack put on his hat. "I'm gonna see if I can round up a sample to compare. Don't go anywhere."

"No worries, I wouldn't miss this for the world."

In the hall, Zack rang Jimmy but got no answer. He walked to the front desk, caught the eye of Officer Brown. "Heard anything from Lieutenant Chaparral, Alex?"

Brown shook his head. "Nope. It's been another quiet morning on the Rez."

"Well, that's good. I'm going out to look for him. If he happens to call, please have him call me."

Zack strode out the door. On his way he tried the call again.

This time, Jimmy answered right away.

"Where are you?" Zack asked.

"I'm just leaving the Hopi Legacy. What's up?"

"Have you found Naatnish yet?"

"It's turning out to be harder than expected. No one seems to know where the man lives."

Zack felt a stir of concern at those words. "Where are you going?"

"Danny Kykotsa suggested I ask Emma about him. I called her, no answer. I'm gonna try to find her."

"Stay there at the hotel, Jimmy. I'm coming to you."

It took five minutes to drive to the Legacy. Jimmy was on the sidewalk. He came over to the Jeep when Zack pulled up. "Got any news?"

"Not so much news as something to try. Hop in."

Jimmy settled into the front seat. Zack spun the wheel and drove out of the lot headed south into Moenkopi. "Did you find where she lives?"

"Emma's house is on Tewa Drive Road; a right, a left, and a second left."

The streets here were laid out like many housing developments, a trunk road with cul-de-sacs on each branch. Emma lived on one of them. They found it right away. The house was kept better than most; it had a nice shade tree protecting the porch from the western sun. Three vehicles sat alongside the house. Zack figured one of them might actually run.

He stood back and let Jimmy knock on the door. The only thing worse than an unannounced Navajo at a Hopi door was a white FBI agent. It didn't matter, as it turned out. Nobody answered.

Zack left Jimmy to keep trying. He stepped off the porch, walked over to the vehicles. Of the three, the Chevy pickup was the only one with enough inflated tires to go anywhere. Zack touched the hood; it was cold. Around back, he found a small garden, a green patch surrounded by red hard-packed dirt. There was a dilapidated shed, its door hanging open. He noticed the garden had been watered recently.

CAT

Zack climbed the three steps up to the tiny back porch. The back door was ajar an inch or so. He nudged it further, called Emma's name. His voice rang off the walls––there was no answer. He peered down a long hallway; saw Jimmy at the front door. He called again. The house appeared empty.

There was a doorway to his left, a bathroom. It was tidy, everything in place. Floral towels, candles, scented soap—all suggested a woman. A hairbrush lay on the mirror shelf. It was similar to the brush he owned, a common type, he guessed. On impulse, he took several strands of hair from it, put them in a Ziploc bag. Might as well check them out.

Outside, Zack shook his head at Jimmy's question. "Nobody home, no sign of a disturbance. Someone must have been here recently to water the garden, though." He climbed into the Jeep. "We can come back later."

Jimmy slid into the other seat. "She's my only clue to finding that old man."

"What about the museum?"

"They don't know. No one bothered to learn where he lives."

Zack threw the Jeep in gear. They lurched forward. "How does he get around, I wonder?"

"That's exactly what George and I were wondering."

CHAPTER THIRTY-ONE

Eagle Feather reached into his pocket for the special bullets when he came near the hogan. He ejected the cartridges already in the rifle, and put the new ones in their place, all the while keeping his eyes on the door. The hogan's unblinking window stared enigmatically.

Rifle ready, he eased toward the building with silent steps. His initial approach had been soundless, he believed, and surprise should be on his side. He decided to press the advantage.

He reached the door, thrust it open, lunged inside. Later an order of things would come to mind—now they seemed to happen all at once—the sudden darkness, the feeling of open space, dirt under his feet, light from a hole above, the sudden frantic flapping of large wings in his face, the screeches, a foul smell in his nose, dust filling the air, the circle of light above blocked, a last pulse of wings. Silence.

He didn't move, waited for his heart to slow, let his eyes adjust. Rays of light from the smoke hole above sifted through floating particles of dust. He saw a fire pit, near it a broken wooden chair, bird shit dripped from it like white icing. The floor was littered with small bones, gleams of white against dark earth. Owl pellets were everywhere. Eagle Feather crinkled his nose in disgust.

He had surprised the great horned owl that lived here with his sudden entrance. It was evident no human had occupied this hogan for years. Eagle Feather guessed the rumors of ghostly inhabitants were likely inspired by the owl's hoots and chuckles, or by its shadow passing overhead.

He went outside for a breath of fresh air. The mountain lion tracks, the barefoot human prints were still there. They were real. They were the true mystery. He studied the arid valley, looked east toward the cliffs where he had been, south to the creek notch, north to the long stretch of barren sand dotted with mesquite and creosote brush, beyond it the bluffs. This place was as desolate as it gets.

Eagle Feather walked a wide circle around the hogan. Behind it he found tracks of many animals, drawn to isolated pools of water in the streambed, but no mountain lion tracks, no human prints.

There was nothing more to learn here. He had found where the lion tracks ended. It was time to learn where they began.

CHAPTER THIRTY-TWO

A man sat in Libby's rocker on the corner of the porch. He had appeared this morning, said Lieutenant Chaparral sent him to watch over the place. Libby figured Zack arranged it; his conscience nagged him, no doubt.

Zack just didn't get it, to her mind. In a way, this was worse than having no one to protect her. It was Zack's way to placate her, sooth his conscience and do exactly what he wanted at the same time. She wondered who would pay for this gesture. The taxpayers? Great.

Libby invited the Navajo in for tea. He politely refused. During the day the man spent his time either on the porch or on patrol around the house and barn. He carried a rifle at all times. His small daypack, a water bottle and a pair of field glasses rested next to the rocker.

Libby spent her day as she often did, caring for the animals, play time with Bernie, doing laundry, a little baking, naptime. She did her barn work while Bernie slept, thought about dinner preparations. Should she make enough for Zack? He hadn't called. Libby had no idea when he'd be home, if at all. She wasn't about to call him. Well, she'd go ahead and make plenty of food. If Zack didn't return in time, she'd feed her expensive babysitter.

It was another crisp October afternoon. The gathering shadows hastened the cold, the sun's heat faded early. It was nippy in the barn; the horses' breath came like mini geysers, the dogs curled tight on their blankets. It felt good to fork hay, kept the circulation pumping. When the barn chores were done, Libby always felt invigorated.

She greeted her guard when she came to the porch, asked him if he needed anything. He shook his head no.

Bernie was still asleep. Libby took advantage and preheated the oven, peeled the potatoes for roasting. Once they were in, she seasoned the pork loin, had just sent it to join the potatoes when she heard Bernie's voice. He liked to talk to himself when he awakened.

She went to his room and they played. The timing worked out well; the roast was in, nothing to do until it was time to steam the vegetables. The half hour with Bernie flew by, as it always did.

Libby returned to the kitchen and put water to boil in the steamer, added the vegetables. She checked the roast. Everything would be ready in half an hour.

Still no word from Zack—no surprise. It was time to invite her babysitter to dinner. She went out to the front porch. The guard was asleep, his chin down on his chest. Poor man. He had had an exhausting day.

"Dinner in half an hour," Libby said, her voice cheery yet brusque. She was not about to accept no for an answer, with all that food. The guard slept on. She was tempted to leave him, let him have his moment of rest, but she figured he should eat.

She went over to the rocker and gently shook his shoulder. His reaction surprised her. He doubled over at the waist, his shoulder fell toward her, his head flopped to one side. Libby could see his throat now, choked off a scream. It gaped open, blood poured from it. The man was dead.

Libby stared, her hands went to her mouth, she fought back screams. She fell back, frantic, eyes searching everywhere. Fighting panic, she backed to the open door, rushed through it and locked it behind her, fastened the chain, threw the bolt, turned on the security system and all the outside lights. She ran to Bernie's room, scooped him up from his crib amid protests, and carried him to the kitchen.

The kitchen was part of the original homestead designed by her grandfather as a blockhouse for defense against warring Indians and roving bands of outlaws. It was the only room in the house with solid wood shutters. The door was the original exterior door, thick, solid, with a sliding bar. She closed the door and barred it.

Bernie continued his protest when she put him in his chair. She absently promised him a treat and spoke to him as she went around to the kitchen windows, closed and secured each one. When Libby went to shutter the window beyond the sink, she stiffened. A lone wolf stood in the fading light of the meadow, exactly where it had been before. It stared at the house, the window—at her.

CHAPTER THIRTY-THREE

"At least we know where Emma is not," Jimmy said. "She's not at the trailer out at Tohnali Spring, it's a crime scene now."

Zack shot him a look. "Your friend Danny had no idea where Naatnish lives?"

Jimmy shook his head. "No one seems to know. I left my number with George Bookbinder. He promised to call me when Nate comes in." He shook his head again, looked frustrated. "I think we're at a dead end for now. We have to wait for both Nate and Emma to turn up." He glanced at Zack. "Drop me off by my vehicle at the hotel, if you don't mind. I need to go check in at the office. I'll keep trying to reach Emma."

It was nearing four when Zack left the Legacy. After a quick stop at the lab to drop off the hair samples, he figured he'd be home in plenty of time for dinner. He could sure use some credit with Libby.

The inevitable messages awaited him at his desk; a few required an immediate response. Alex was already gone. His note said, "Good day today. No hanging chads. Enjoy your evening. Alex."

Well, that's good, anyway, Zack thought. He sighed.

By the time he climbed back into the Jeep, the sun was close to the horizon. In another forty-five minutes he approached the house. It was full dark now. As he drove up the circular stone driveway the Jeep headlights swept the front porch. A man sat in Libby's rocker.

Zack slammed on the brakes, let his headlights shine on him. Ah, the guard, he remembered, feeling grateful to Jimmy. Yet, something about the man seemed strange, he apparently was asleep. Zack looked at the way he slumped against the chair arm, head hanging. Something black glistened in the light. It was all over the man's shoulder, on the chair arm. It must be blood. Now he saw the black line across the man's pale throat.

Panic surged through him, yet Zack's brain absorbed critical details; the outside spots were on, the barn lights were on too. Whatever happened, Libby had time to throw the switch. His eyes flew to the door. A tiny red light pulsated above it. The security system was turned on.

Zack sat in the Jeep, engine running, tried to think. He had to assume Libby and Bernie were safe inside. His eyes went back to the body. The man's rifle leaned against his leg, on its stock. He hadn't had time to pick it up. Had he fallen asleep? Or was the killer so crafty, so quick. Zack realized his own life could be in danger each second he sat there.

He levered the Jeep into four-wheel drive, popped the clutch, lurched forward, and gunned the engine. If the killer wasn't inside, he must be lurking in the shadows somewhere around the house. Zack needed to go on the offensive.

CAT

The vehicle careened across the drive, accelerating, slammed into the sloped embankment of the lawn. The front wheels rebounded, lifted, the Jeep flew up and over, landing in the side yard. Zack fought for control, spun the steering wheel toward the house, the Jeep came around. He put on high beams, accelerated along the building, the headlights shown on the side of the house, the low decorative bushes, the meadow beyond. No one was there.

The rear corner of the building flew toward him, he kept his foot on the accelerator, pulled up the handbrake, whipped the steering wheel hard. The back end of the vehicle slid around, tearing up turf. The headlights swung onto the back wall.

Part way down, at the baby's window, a figure had hands on the windowsill. Now it turned to look, its eyes glowed in the headlights. Zack saw a wolf's head with a toothy snarling mouth.

He gunned the Jeep, raced toward the figure. The thing ran with incredible quickness out of the headlights into the meadow. Zack jammed on the brakes, careened the Jeep around to follow. The high beams swung across the meadow, bleached the tall grass white with their light. There was nothing there—the thing had vanished.

The bastard can't get away, not now. Zack left the engine running in neutral, pulled on the handbrake, dug his handgun out of the glove compartment, ripped the hand torch from its mount, and leapt out of the jeep. He ran into the meadow into the headlights, his giant shadow leading him.

The thing could not have reached the tree line so quickly, must be lying prone in the grass here somewhere. Handgun out, safety off, Zack ran hard, played the torch from side to side.

Halfway to the fence line, a sudden thought stopped him. He was playing into the killer's hands. He was running too far from the house. He could not allow the killer to circle behind and threaten his family.

Zack turned, ran back toward the building, past the idling Jeep with its lights glowing across the meadow. He checked Bernie's window; it appeared undamaged. No one replied to his shouts, there was no chance for anyone inside the house to hear him over the Jeep engine, the noise of the panicked animals, the shriek of the security alarm.

He ran around the house, bounded up the porch steps, fumbled for his key and unlocked the front door. Once inside he relocked it, yelled Libby's name. A muffled reply came from the kitchen.

Zack pulled out his phone and dialed 911. He left a terse message. "This is FBI Special Agent Zack Tolliver. Officer under attack, please respond. Jimmy Chaparral, your man is dead, my house is under attack, get help out here now."

He ran to the kitchen, leaned his face against the thick kitchen door. "Libby, I'm here. You can let me in." He heard a reply, heard the bar begin to slide.

The low rumbling background sound of the Jeep engine suddenly changed. Zack stopped to listen. He heard the vehicle move away. The engine sound changed again, this time with rising RPMs until it screamed at a high pitch. The sound grew louder. Zack realized the vehicle was coming toward the house at high speed.

He yelled, "Wait, wait, Libby," heard the bar stop its slide. At the same time there was a tremendous impact, the living room wall buckled, wood cracked like pistol shots, window glass shattered, the roaring of the Jeep engine filled the room, a smell of gasoline and hot engine oil grew strong.

The log home's sturdy construction kept the vehicle mostly out, but there were large gaps between timbers where they bent and cracked inward. The living room window casement was fragmented, the glass blown out.

The wolf's head figure appeared in the window opening. Zack fired at it, kept firing until it withdrew. He was sure his shots were on target, but took no chances.

"Libby, stay there. Don't come out." He waited, crouched by the wall, ready. His Glock held a dozen more bullets. The security siren wailed on, the smell of gasoline grew much stronger. The logs must be soaked in it, Zack realized. Almost immediately, flames appeared.

The fire extinguisher was barricaded in the kitchen with Libby. No help there. He sprinted to the bathroom, ran water in the tub, took a large towel and soaked it with water. He raced back with it, flung it over the flaming logs, ran back for another. It was critical to put out the fire before it reached the gas tank. He soaked more towels, beat the flames with them, draped them over the burning wood. Slowly the flames diminished.

The security siren stopped wailing, the fire must have melted a wire. The sudden stillness was deafening. It was the only reason he heard the shattering of glass in Bernie's room.

Zack ran there, gun in hand. He dove through the door, sliding on his side along the floor, both hands gripping the Glock while firing at the window. The wolf's head jerked away. Somehow Zack knew the nine-millimeter bullets wouldn't kill it.

The fire. He must get back to it, make sure it was out. He sprinted to the living room. As he ran, the thought came—that's what he expects me to do. Instead, Zack ran to the fireplace, pulled down the shotgun from the mantle. It was an 1897 Winchester 12 gauge that Libby's dad had owned. Shells for it were in the drawer of the gun cabinet. Zack found them, broke the gun open, fumbled with the shells, loaded both barrels, and ran back to Bernie's room.

He was in time to see the figure swing a leg inside the window. The creature was entirely encased in fur, the wolf's head worn on its head like a hat. Angry red eyes glared at him, the wolf's head mouth set in a snarl.

Zack raised the shotgun, aimed carefully, and fired point blank. The man-creature moved with astonishing quickness but could not avoid the buckshot. It impacted its upper chest, blew through the fur that covered it, exposed red-pitted raw flesh. The man-thing disappeared.

CAT

No time to pursue it now. To the bathroom, another towel, back to the fire. More trips with soaking towels until Zack was sure the fire was out. Only then was he aware of flashing red and blue lights outside the house.

Zack slumped against the kitchen door. "Libby, you can come out now," he said.

CHAPTER THIRTY-FOUR

Eagle Feather retraced his steps until he came to where he had crossed the lion tracks, and began to backtrack them. The prints led him toward the opposite cliffs, across the barren sand among the sparse sage. He tracked them across the bone-dry creek bed, where they were clear and deep in the sand.

A small patch of grass in the shade of some cottonwood trees on the opposite bank looked too inviting to resist. Eagle Feather rested and swigged some water. He absorbed his surroundings; the bush studded terra cotta flatland and the fortress-like cliffs guarding it. No buildings, no highways, no billboards, just the valley as it had always been—as it should remain, in his opinion. Yet beneath the surface of this serene world an ancient evil existed, its own harmful spirits hovered. It will always be so, Eagle Feather thought.

After he left his patch of shade, Eagle Feather found the prints easy to follow, once again in sand and clay yielding good impressions. The tracks led from the southwest in a straight line. He thought the lion had come from the cliffs west of the creek gorge.

He was right. An hour later the prints led him to an ancient trail up a steep arroyo, toward the top of the bluffs. It followed a natural cleft in the sandstone. Several yards from the summit, the rim rock had collapsed, requiring Eagle Feather to scramble to reach the top.

CAT

He paused there, rested on a moonscape of smooth sandstone. It covered the mesa top, with crevices here and there; the sandstone slightly rounded between the cracks like a series of turtle shells. There was no trail to follow, no prints; feet left no impression on this hard, wind-weathered surface.

The mesa sloped away west until it disappeared from sight in the Hamblin Wash. The lowering sun created a sparkling river across the reflective rock surface. Dusk would come soon.

Eagle Feather was uncomfortable here, felt exposed, sky-lined for anyone to see. This high ground was not the place to camp. He trotted south, parallel to the cliffs, his pace rapid across the smooth rock surface.

He noted familiar landmarks far below, the Willow Creek gorge, the wider basin beyond. He could even see his truck far across the valley, a tiny blip of red among the boulders.

His progress came to an abrupt end when the ground fell away in front of him. A great arroyo hundreds of feet deep crossed his path. He turned west and walked along the rim toward the head, came to a place where weathered steps carved in the sandstone descended the cliff face out of sight. They were Anasazi hand and foot holds, worn round and smooth over the centuries, not an inviting prospect, to Eagle Feather's mind. Further on the rock surface he trod had been worn smooth by many feet. The arroyo dwindled to a narrow crack, in it a cave-like hollow. Eagle Feather thought this must be the place Jimmy Chaparral described.

A Navajo by birth and nurture, Eagle Feather felt uncomfortable around Anasazi ruins. The word Anasazi meant "ancient enemy" in the Navajo language. *Chindi,* such as the one Lori Welkai had seen, were often associated with such sites. That was bad.

He stole a glance at the horizon. With no more than two hours before dusk he had no desire to be anywhere near this place after dark. On the other hand, if he left without exploring the area for signs of recent activity, this entire outing would be to no purpose. Eagle Feather decided to make a quick survey, maybe ten minutes, twenty at the most, and be gone.

With his rifle strapped to the top of his pack, both hands free, he scrambled down to the floor of the hollow. Light entered through the fissure above and behind him. In its glow two black handprints stood out on the wall ahead, as bold and perfect as if placed there yesterday. Beyond, the cave floor sloped away, a sandstone slide that disappeared from sight, as Jimmy had described.

Eagle Feather dug out the equipment he packed for the purpose—forty meters of light crevasse rescue rope, a harness, rock hammer, pitons, an ascender/rappel device, and several carabiners.

He drove a piton into the rock as close to the lip as he dared go, attached a locking 'biner, and set up his rappel. Like most climbers, he was not excited about blind rappels, but especially not into a site crawling with spirits.

CAT

He tried to put those thoughts out of his mind and concentrate on his technique.

As it turned out, the rappel was short and easy, the angle forgiving, the rock surface smooth all the way down. He landed on a three-foot ledge in the arroyo wall several hundred feet above the ground. The ledge traversed the cliff for fifty feet, ended where a ladder leaned against the wall. Eagle Feather remained secured to his rope, used it to creep along the ledge.

He came into shadow. An ancient ladder led up to a large cave mouth. The ladder was constructed of tree branches fastened by sinew; it looked like the original. Eagle Feather's rope had run out. He would have to chance this climb without protection.

The ladder had five rungs. The dry sinew ties looked secure, despite their age. He climbed with care, placed his weight gently on each rung, his hands on the rock face to redistribute his weight. After all these centuries, the ladder held.

Eagle Feather stood at the cave mouth, in awe of the buildings before him. This was the most intact Anasazi ruin he'd ever seen. But for the layer of undisturbed dust, it felt as if the inhabitants might be back any moment.

He entered, walked among towering mud-brick dwellings, flashlight in hand. The passageway through them was narrow, bounded by the building walls. Keyhole doorways and gaping windows were dark, secretive. It was unnerving, as if residents even now peered out at him.

The long passage brought him to an open area, a plaza of sorts, surrounded by more buildings and passageways. In the center of the plaza he saw the familiar kiva, an underground ceremonial room found in every Anasazi dwelling. Unlike most kivas, this one had an intact roof. Eagle Feather could see the top of a wood ladder project above the wood-framed hatch.

Tiny rodent and bird tracks wandered through the layer of powdery dust. He found no other prints—no humans, no mountain lions. He was relieved. His mission was accomplished; he could leave this place.

A glance at his watch told him he still had time. He walked the circumference of the plaza, found the dust undisturbed. All that was left for him now was check the kiva. He put a tentative foot on the roof, leaned forward to look in. It held, seemed solid.

Disaster came suddenly. The roof cracked, his foot broke through before he could withdraw it, penetrated up to his thigh. Dried mud and wattle rained to the dirt floor beneath. The kiva roof sagged, groaned, gave way. Eagle Feather dropped to the kiva floor, landed on his back, the air forced from his lungs. Debris piled on top of him.

When he could breathe again, he opened his eyes. It was dark here. He tested his body, one limb at a time. Nothing broken. He'd lost the flashlight when he fell, he searched for it now, his head turning incrementally parsing the darkness. There it was, a tiny glow. He crawled toward it, his knees and palms pressing into sharp objects along the way. The flashlight was under a pile of debris. He dug it out, it still worked, but the flurry of suspended dust particles in the air blunted its reach. The tiny beam showed him high, smooth walls that looked un-climbable. Eagle Feather stood to gauge the height of the kiva roof. The original hatchway, enlarged by his fall, was not large enough to be helpful. The opening remained several feet removed from the wall and ten or twelve feet above, well out of reach. The ladder was completely broken. It was going to be very difficult to get out.

He could see nothing above and beyond the kiva but a lighter shade of darkness. The ghostly village was as still as death. He probed the walls of his prison with the flashlight, explored the floor. He found decorative corrugated earthenware pots, bits of dried animal skin, leather pouches, painted gourds, and woodcarvings—all under a thick layer of dust and debris. In the very center was the ceremonial *sipapu*, a circular hole about five inches in diameter, access for the gods, as he remembered.

Beyond it, something reflected his light beam. He moved the flashlight across it, stared, recognized it—a human skull. At the same moment he heard a strange hollow booming sound, a single percussive drum-like noise. It echoed off the cave walls, the sound reaching down into his kiva prison from the ruins above.

CHAPTER THIRTY-FIVE

Jimmy Chaparral had just returned from the privy behind the police station when he noticed that the 911 emergency message light was blinking. He pushed the button. Before Zack's words had stopped pouring out from the recording he had already buckled on his holster belt, grabbed the shotgun from the wall, and was out the door. The Blazer tires spun. He listened to the police radio as he drove.

A state trooper near Cameron, closer to Zack's house, would respond right away, to Jimmy's relief.

The 45-minute drive to Cameron from Elk Wells took half an hour. That was fast, but it felt slow. It felt even slower when he came up behind a pokey out-of-state driver just beyond Cameron on Route 64. The tourist was blind to his lights, deaf to his siren. Another time, he'd have pulled him over on suspicion of driving while stupid. Instead, he rode up on his bumper until the man got out of his way.

Jimmy barely slowed at the turn to Zack's house, took to the air several times off bumps on the secondary road. As he pulled up to the driveway he saw the flashing lights of two patrol cars. The house front door stood open, exterior spotlights were on. A cacophony of sounds came from the animals in the barn.

Jimmy sprinted up the porch steps. When he saw Bob, his volunteer guard, draped over the arm of a rocker, blood pooled on the porch floorboards, he stopped short.

CAT

A trooper stood by the body, taking notes. Jimmy didn't need to go any closer to see Bob was dead. He felt guilt, then anger. He rushed on, burst into the living room.

The scene here was one of chaos. Water pooled on the floor and soaked the rugs, glass shards glistened and twinkled everywhere. The far living room wall caved inward, plaster hung by paper strips or was crushed underfoot into powdery mud. The thick wall support beams were cracked, window frames distorted and broken. A vehicle bumper protruded into the room, much of the wood near it charred. The place was a mess.

Jimmy looked around wildly. He saw Libby in the big chair, Bernie in her lap. A trooper stood near her, notebook in hand. She glanced up when he approached.

"What the..." Jimmy tried to speak, couldn't get words out.

"We're okay. But your poor man on the porch..."

"What the hell happened here?"

Libby was pale, her eyes wide. Bernie was asleep, somehow. Before she could reply, Jimmy found his voice. "My God, are you alright? Can I get you some water, tea, anything? Where's Zack?"

Libby almost smiled at his panic. "No, thank you, we're fine. I don't want to wake up Bernie. Zack is out behind the house looking for whoever it was attacked us. He shot him several times, he wants to be sure he's dead. Go find him, talk to him. He can tell you more."

Jimmy rested a hand on her shoulder, did as he was told. Out on the porch, he walked over to Bob's body. The man's throat was cut deep, neck almost severed.

"He must have dozed off, the killer crept up behind him. The poor guy likely died before he even knew what happened," the trooper said.

Jimmy nodded. He spoke into his radio, asked who was responding. The dispatcher told him the Navajo Nation Police from Tuba City were already on their way, bringing their forensic unit.

Jimmy went around to the side of the house. In the light of the security floods he saw Zack's red Jeep at an angle, its front end through the exterior wall of the house, the whole business pushed in. A third state trooper inspecting the vehicle looked up at Jimmy's approached. He raised an eyebrow at him.

Jimmy flashed his badge. "Lieutenant Jim Chaparral, Navajo Nation Police. I'm out of the Elk Wells office. I'm also a friend of the residents."

"Trooper Rondell," the man said. "Agent Tolliver went out there." He gestured toward the meadow. "He's looking for the perp's body."

Jimmy looked out where the security light ended and night began. "He's dead?"

"Tolliver seems to think so. Said he saw the buckshot hit the guy's chest."

"I'm going to back him up, just in case." Jimmy took his flashlight from his belt, walked out into the meadow where the trooper indicated. He could see a swale through the tall grass and a lot of blood. The killer couldn't survive long, he thought.

He walked on. As if to deliberately contradict him, the blood trail began to thin out. Jimmy was surprised. The killer had managed to staunch the flow somehow.

A split rail fence loomed up. Jimmy climbed over it, found Zack's prints on the other side. He followed them into the trees, there the trail stopped. The woods were thick and dark. The forest floor and undergrowth gave nothing away to the light of his flashlight. It was impossible to track here.

Unable to see where to go, Jimmy turned back, stopped when he heard sounds from the nearby brush, saw branches move.

"Hold your fire, it's me, Agent Tolliver."

"Zack, its Jimmy."

Zack's familiar figure came into view. They stared at each other. "I am very glad you came," Zack said. "Did you see Libby?"

"Libby and Bernie are fine. The troopers are with them."

"We better go back. I lost the guy, I wouldn't put it past him to circle back behind me."

"Libby said you hit him. I saw a lot of blood."

Zack shook his head, puzzled. "I hit him several times with the Glock, once with a twelve gauge." Zack turned toward the house, spoke as he walked. "He shouldn't be alive. It's remotely possible I missed with the handgun, but I know I hit him in the middle of the chest with the twelve-gauge. I saw the impact."

They walked together through the meadow. The log home and barn blazed with light, swirling red and blue flashes reflected on the buildings and trees. It was quiet now. With the alarm off, people no longer rushing around, the animals had gradually calmed down. From this perspective it was like a scene from a silent movie.

Zack grabbed Jimmy's arm. "I don't want Libby upset beyond her present state. As far as we know, my shot killed the guy and he crawled off into the woods to die. We'll look for the body tomorrow. You okay with that?"

Jimmy smiled at Zack, shook his head. "Good luck with that. You never could lie very well."

CHAPTER THIRTY-SIX

Eagle Feather's flashlight revealed several skulls in a row. They faced the *sipapu*, jaws agape with monstrous grins as if amused by the irony of death.

The shades of night grew darker yet. His luminous watch dial said 6:30 pm, but it might as well be midnight in this deep well of a prison.

Another muffled boom echoed off the cave walls above. It startled Eagle Feather; it came so long after the first he'd almost forgotten. He couldn't tell how far apart they were. Down here, it felt as if time itself was devoured by the impenetrable blackness.

Eagle Feather studied the wall of the kiva. It was hacked out of sandstone, buffed smooth, a mortar-like substance applied over all. It offered no grip. Even if he could climb it, the center hatch would be well out of his reach. The entrance hole, though now considerably wider after his breakthrough, offered no trailing timber or sinew to grasp to help him escape. There was nothing on the floor sufficiently tall to stand on to reach the top. Eagle Feather was forced to conclude he had no way out.

He heard a third boom—measured, muffled. Someone, something must be in the ruin with him. Eagle Feather's thoughts went to *chindi*, witches, or worse, despite reason. Right now he found small comfort in logical thought.

His guide experience taught him to focus on basic details first. He took inventory of his belongings. There was the flashlight, for as long as the battery held out, and the handgun. It was a snub nose .38 Smith & Wesson police special, a seldom-used weapon; he probably couldn't hit the side of a barn with it. It was fully loaded, had six bullets, but no extra cartridges. Along with his rifle, he had plenty of firepower.

The Navajo guide always carried a sheath knife with a four and a half inch blade. It even had a bottle opener on it, if he only had a bottle to open. He had water and a sandwich. There was his slicker to use as a blanket if he got cold, and matches. Eagle Feather didn't want to be in this hole, but at least he was equipped to survive the night. Hopefully, daylight would reveal a way to escape. He glanced at his watch. It had been four minutes since the last drum sound. Maybe the ghost drummer was done for the night.

Eagle Feather thought about a fire. The dried sapling, chunks of branch, pieces of hide and sinew from the fractured ceiling were all very dry. They wouldn't burn for long, but the fire would be bright, and later the coals would keep him warm for a while and save the batteries in his flashlight. He gathered up the debris.

When he touched the pile with a match, it flared up instantly. The interior of the kiva brightened, the row of skulls grinned at him. He lay back on his slicker, his pack a pillow. His eyes drifted up to the hole in the kiva roof.

CAT

The firelight glistened on a pair of green orbs—eyes, focused on him. He stiffened, his small hairs rose. He saw the vague outline of a huge mountain lion crouched just beyond the widened kiva mouth, ready to leap.

Without thought Eagle Feather reached for the rifle with his right hand, brought it across his body, rotated to point it up at the lion. He waited. The green orbs stared back, unblinking.

At a loss for any other tactic, he spoke to the creature, his tone conversational despite his fear. "Well, kitty, you have a choice to make. You can jump down here and take a 30-30 shell to the chest or you can stay up there and be safe. If you are more than a cat, you better know a shaman dipped these bullets in ash at a special ceremony. I guess you know what that means. It's your move." Somehow, Eagle Feather felt better at the sound of his own voice.

The green eyes stared. Eagle Feather stared back. He was sure he didn't blink or look away, yet a moment later the cat was gone. He released his breath.

His mind raced back over the events of the day. The mountain lion must have hidden somewhere near the hogan, followed him back here. Now it was in the ruin and had him trapped like a bug in a bottle. All things considered, he'd rather see it manifest above him than wonder where it was, or when it might leap down on him.

To his mind, he couldn't maintain this position all night, so he rearranged, tried lying on his back, the rifle stock planted on the ground by his side, its barrel pointed up. The handgun went close by. There might be time for one rifle shot, after that he'd need the handgun and the knife. His arm cuddled around the rifle, Eagle Feather drank some water, and munched on the sandwich. It was going to be a long night.

CHAPTER THIRTY-SEVEN

Zack drove Libby and Bernie away from the ranch in the pickup. Libby was still in shock, Bernie asleep. They passed through the east entrance of the national park, drove along Desert View Drive all the way to South Entrance Road. Zack tried to get Libby to talk. She didn't respond.

They turned south on the entrance road to the small village of Tusayan. Zack took a room at the Grand Hotel. In the lobby, with its thick wooded beams and soaring ceiling, the comfortable hum of chatter at the bar, the occasional guest passing by, there was a feeling of normalcy that appeared to comfort Libby. She and Bernie would be safe here.

Zack stayed the night, ate breakfast with his family. Libby had little to say; he guessed she blamed him for the attack on their home. He didn't have an answer.

He left them here, returned to the ranch, now a crime scene. The state boys crawled all over the place. The Navajo Nation Police and the FBI were all involved. Since Zack was considered a victim in this case, he would not participate in the investigation. He'd have to learn what he could from Jimmy.

The morning was clear and cold, a thin coat of snow twinkled in the early sun. Zack had plenty of time to think. He had to admit it was difficult not to give credence to the skinwalker idea, yet he resisted. Even if the pistol bullets missed their target, which he doubted, the shotgun had hit its mark. How could a man survive that, let alone run away, escape? Maybe it was the shotgun shells. They were as old as the gun, might have lost explosiveness over the years. The gunpowder might have degraded.

The house droned with activity. Tape was strung everywhere. Zack had to identify himself several times just to get to the barn to feed the animals. An FBI agent found him there forking hay, interviewed him as he worked.

Zack talked about his fortuitous arrival home, the dead guard, his battle to ward off the assailant, his attempt to track him later. When he finished, he mentioned the unseen intruder two nights prior.

"The Navajo Nation Police lieutenant from Elk Wells, Jim Chaparral, was here after that first incident," Zack said. "He knows the whole story."

The agent snapped his notebook closed. "Excellent. I'll have a chat with him." He turned to go, paused. "I'll need to talk to your wife, too."

Zack produced a card from his shirt pocket, gave it to him. "She's staying at this hotel for the time being. She's expecting you."

Jimmy came into the barn as Zack finished up his chores. He perched on a hay bale, watched. "That FBI honcho spoke with you, I guess."

"Yep."

"Did you tell him about Emma and Amå and all that?"

"Nope. I figure that's your case."

Jimmy grinned. "Can't blame you for not opening that can of worms."

Zack grimaced. "I didn't care to explain why I was hanging out in graveyards in the middle of the night." He leaned on his broom. "Has anyone tried to find the killer this morning?"

"I went out there first thing." Jimmy said. "I found your tracks, followed them, saw where you turned around. I didn't find any trace of the guy beyond there."

"I didn't either."

"But.. "

"But what?"

Jimmy stared at the ground. "I kept walking in the same general direction. A couple of hundred yards on I found a wolf track." He glanced up at Zack. "It was a big animal. The print was made last night some time. Coincidence, I suppose."

Zack eyed him, said nothing.

Jimmy went on. "The *yee naaldlooshii*, the skinwalker, is hard to kill, but if wounded it will carry the same wound in the same place on his human body." Jimmy raised an eyebrow at Zack. "All we have to do is find a suspect with a shotgun wound to his chest."

Zack didn't smile. "He should be dead."

Jimmy stood. "I'm gonna go back and talk to everyone all over again. Emma, Danny, Lori, George Bookbinder, even Naatnish, if I can find him. I'll be looking for anyone who might have a new chest wound."

Zack eyed him. "That's your plan?"

175

Jimmy laughed. "You go back to your shiny lab, your DNA, your blood analysis. We'll see

CHAPTER THIRTY-EIGHT

Eagle Feather sensed it was dawn from a slight change in the quality of darkness, nothing more. It wouldn't be long before he had enough light to look for a way out of his prison. The cave above him faced east; once the sun was high enough, its rays should strike the cave mouth and lighten the interior.

The night had been long. Eagle Feather's knees ached from crouching, his neck had a crick from looking up, the rifle had grown anvil heavy in his hand. He dared not release it even for a moment.

The lion had visited several times in the night, hoping to find him asleep and unaware, was his guess. He saw the green glow of its eyes each time, called to it—*Come on, kitty, come on down. I've got a welcome for you.* After a while, it would vanish; he never did see it go.

With the dawn would come Eagle Feather's best chance to escape. He would no longer need his flashlight to see, and if the lion was more than a lion, it should vanish with the morning light. If it was just a mountain lion, he didn't fear it. Either way, his opportunity to escape would come soon—or never.

The night in the kiva had been terrifying in many ways. The booming drumbeat came at unexpected moments; sometimes single strokes separated by long intervals, sometimes a sudden frenzied pounding, at which time Eagle Feather's heart would race along with it as if biologically linked. There had been other noises, distant whispers, rustlings, snapping; there had been shadows whisping by above.

These things did not surprise Eagle Feather. He expected them here in this place. Still, he feared them. The *chindi* associated with this village of the dead were a danger to him.

The intrusion of dawn's light was slow, almost imperceptible. Eagle Feather fought sleep. The early hours were the hardest. He waited to act until he could distinguish objects in the kiva without the aid of the flashlight.

The broken kiva ladder was his only hope. A section of the sidepiece was cracked beyond repair. In the new light the roof opening seemed closer, might not require as much ladder length as he first thought. Eagle Feather dug in his pack for his etrier, made of thin but tough cord, previously tied off into three steps. He'd have to sacrifice it. He cut the cord in multiple pieces and began the tedious task of rebuilding the ladder. He had to omit a rung. His finished project was little more than ten feet tall. To his relief, when he stood it up, it just reached the lowest portion of the roof.

Eagle Feather eyed the ladder and the roof supporting it. Neither gave him confidence. He repacked his gear, strapped on the rifle, pulled on his pack and faced the ladder. After a deep breath, he climbed. His weight pushed the top of the ladder against the roofing. It gave way, bit by bit like dominoes falling, but the downward slope of the roof was just enough to support the top of the ladder as it broke through. Eagle Feather climbed fast so not to let his full weight settle on any one rung. Moments later he was on solid ground. The roof disintegrated behind him in a cloud of dust, mud, and wattle. The reconstructed ladder with his etrier cord was now at the bottom of the kiva. He hoped he wouldn't need it to ascend the cliff.

His escape was noisy. The lion couldn't help but hear if it was still around.

Eagle Feather hurried to the cave entranceway. Here the early morning light stripped away the ominous secrets inhabiting the darkness, left simple mud-brick, crumbling buildings in their place. The Navajo guide descended the entrance ladder with care, navigated the narrow ledge. He was relieved to find his rope and equipment still in place. The climb up the smooth steep surface was not difficult, even without the etrier. In the upper cave, he collected his rope, his gear, took off his harness, and packed it all away.

He climbed out by the north wall, at the first try. He remembered Jimmy's story, looked back at the ridgeline where the strange figure of a man had stood, saw nothing.

Groggy from lack of sleep, nerve ends tingling, pain radiating from cuts, bruises and sore muscles; Eagle Feather decided he'd never felt so good in his life.

CHAPTER THIRTY-NINE

Danny Kykotsa was just leaving Emma's house when Jimmy drove up. He pulled his vehicle alongside the Blazer, rolled down his window. "Don't bother; she's not home."

Jimmy was frustrated. "You'd think with Amå gone she'd be around more."

"Maybe now she's not tied to the old lady, she's got a life."

"Around here, huh?" Jimmy smiled, despite his irritation.

"Want me to take a message in case I bump into her?"

"You might ask her to give me a call."

"Will do." Danny drove off.

Jimmy sat idling the Blazer a moment longer. When he last saw Emma, she was planning to prepare a traditional burial for Amå. None but specific mourners were to know where it would take place, only that it would be far enough from the trailer to prevent her *chindi* from returning to it. It would occur as soon as possible, likely that same afternoon. That was two days ago now, and Emma was nowhere to be found. Jimmy thought about Danny's words, grunted to himself. He didn't agree Emma was out kicking up her heels. That did not seem her style.

He parked the Blazer in Emma's driveway. He was here now, might as well take a look around. The front door wasn't latched, it pushed open when he knocked. Someone forgot to close it. He called out. No one home, as Danny said.

Danny. Why had he come here? Jimmy should have asked him. The man had retired when the Hopi Rangers became an official police force, didn't want to go through the new training and the red tape bullshit, as he called it. Still, once a cop, always a cop—it would be like him to come here and sniff around.

Jimmy walked through the empty rooms. Everything was neat as pie, the air stale, like Emma hadn't been here for weeks, let alone days. The kitchen was bare, counters clear, every pan and utensil put away. The little bathroom down the hall was just as neat, the little mirror shelf empty, nothing hanging on hooks. Emma's bedroom was the same. He stepped out on the back porch, stood there for a moment contemplating the back yard. The little garden appeared withered and dry, another indication of the owner's long absence.

He decided there was nothing else to learn here, walked down the hall and out of the house, closed the door firmly behind him. Under the shade tree in front, he took a final look around. Everything appeared just the way it had when he and Zack were here yesterday. The vehicles were in exactly the same place.

Jimmy scratched his head. How was Emma getting around? If she walked place to place, somebody would have seen her. He felt a gnawing worry in his stomach. She had been very close to Amå, now she was all alone. Jimmy did not think Emma would hurt herself; she was too tough for that. Still, there could have been an accident, maybe just after the burial when everyone else was gone.

Jimmy thought about it, shook his head. In that case, how did her truck get back? It was here now—it was here when he and Zack came by, the day after the murder. The engine had been cold then, he remembered.

He sighed. Danny must be right. Emma must have driven the truck home after the burial, hid away somewhere to do some private grieving. There seemed no other answer.

Jimmy's thoughts turned to Naatnish. There was a guy he really wanted to find, see if the man was hiding a chest wound.

He climbed into the Blazer and drove to the Navajo Interpretive Museum. Jimmy hoped Bookbinder might think of something he'd forgotten before.

George was on the museum floor, speaking with guests. After a while, the tourists moved on. Bookbinder noticed the Navajo policeman, walked over to him.

"Those folks were looking for McDonald's, ended up here by mistake. Once they were here, they got curious." George grinned. "I'll take 'em any way I can get 'em."

Jimmy smile back. "I came here to—"

"To see if I've seen Nate since you left. No, I haven't. I did come across an address, though."

Jimmy raised an eyebrow.

"Come with me." Bookbinder led the way to his office.

George pointed to a package on his desk, put his finger on the return address. "Nate borrowed a couple of books a while back, returned them by mail."

Jimmy looked at the printed sticker. It read: "Naatnish Featherman, Hopi Assisted Living, Suite 43, 21 Senior Lane, Tuba City". "

"Assisted Living—of course. Why didn't I think of that?"

Bookbinder held up a cautionary finger. "The man whisps here and there like a ghost, so no guarantees."

"If he's not there now, they should know where to look." Jimmy was already out the door. "Thanks, George."

Senior Lane was off Hopi Drive in Moenkopi, just opposite Tewa Drive, where Emma lived. Coincidence? Jimmy wondered.

When he arrived at the assisted living facility, he inquired at the desk.

The clerk was a perky young Hopi girl. "Sure, Nate lives here. Are you a relative?"

The question surprised Jimmy. "No, I'm a police officer. Why do you ask?"

The girl gave a bright official smile. "Well, the hospital is only allowing close relatives to visit right now."

"The Hospital? What hospital."

"The Tuba City Health Care Center. That's where they took him."

"Whoa, slow down. They took Nate to the hospital? Why?"

"I was told he was complaining of a chest pain."

I'll bet he is, Jimmy thought. "When did they take him in?"

"Early this morning. Just before I came on my shift."

Jimmy thanked her. He pushed his way out through the heavy glass door, stood on the sidewalk, and called Zack.

No answer. He left a message. "I found Naatnish. He is in the Tuba City Health Care Center. Word is it's a chest pain. I'm on my way there now."

CHAPTER FORTY

Zack watched Eagle Feather's rust-red truck pull up behind him in front of the FBI office in Tuba City. He waited on the sidewalk for his friend to unravel from behind the steering wheel. It took a while. The Navajo walked toward him with halting Zombie-like steps.

"You look like shit," Zack said.

"Thanks, White Man."

"No, really, you look like shit. What happened?"

"It's a long story, I am cold, hungry, and I look like shit. Do you mind if we at least go inside with this conversation?"

"Yeah, sure. You can use the lab shower, if you like. Then we can go over to Julia's for a bite."

When they came through the door of the lab, Linda was at her microscope. She glanced up, her eyes widened when she saw Eagle Feather.

"You look like—"

"Yes, yes, I know."

"Eagle Feather needs to use your shower," Zack said.

"Yeah, sure, help yourself. It's all warmed up for you, I was just in it." Linda's eye went back to the microscope.

"I've got a couple of spare shirts in the changing room. Help yourself," Zack said, as Eagle Feather disappeared into the washroom.

When he was gone, Linda looked up at Zack. "What happened to him?"

"He hasn't told me yet. I guess we'll know when he gets out of the shower."

"You must have had quite the night yourself. I was over at your place this morning, the Flagstaff boys called me in. The place was hopping— I was the third forensic team on the scene." Linda chuckled. "All by myself."

"Staties, Navajo, and FBI?"

"Yeah. I'm surprised the National Parks unit wasn't there."

Zack came around the table, pulled out a stool next to her. "What have you found?"

"About what?"

"About last night, for now."

"All kinds of stuff, some of which might even be useful. Blood samples, for example."

"From the bedroom window?"

Linda nodded. "Everyone dipped their swabs there, but I was able to get a nice clean sample. I've sent it out already."

"To Florida?"

She grinned. "Oh, yeah."

"What else?"

"I took swabs from the Navajo guard's neck. The cut was clean, had to be a sharp knife. I've got photos to study. I dusted the Jeep steering wheel and shift lever, but with the fire and water and all, I don't hold out a lot of hope." She peered at Zack with a mischievous smile.

CAT

"Your name is mud at the FBI motor pool. You'll be gettin' around on a mule after this."

"Not for the first time. Work on those prints, will you, so I can prove it wasn't me wrecked it."

"Did you wreck another vehicle, White Man?" Eagle Feather stood at the washroom door, buttoning one of Zack's shirts. The button-down collar was a startling contrast to his dusty black leather pants and long wet hair.

"Never mind that. What happened to you?"

Eagle Feather came over, pulled out a stool. "You want the short version, or the long version?"

"How about the short version, for now. You can give me the longer version over breakfast at Julia's."

Eagle Feather began. At the point the mountain lion tracks turned to barefoot human prints, Linda looked up.

"Here we go."

"Was it a trick?" Zack asked.

Eagle Feather shrugged. "Looked real to me." He went on with his story. Linda gave up all pretenses of work, listened with her chin on her palms.

When his account was done, Eagle Feather looked at Zack.

"I'm waiting for you to say the word skinwalker," Zack said.

"Draw your own conclusions. When I spoke to that lion, told it my bullets were dipped in ash, I was covering all my bases."

"If your lion was the skinwalker and with you all night, as you say, it couldn't have been at my house."

Eagle Feather looked at Zack, puzzled.

"I think you need to hear my story now." Zack said. He told an abbreviated version. When he finished, Eagle Feather looked grim.

"So far that's two murders, and an attempt on you and your family."

"We have no evidence to connect the two murders, at least not yet," Zack said, with a glance at Linda. "As it stands, Amá's murder case belongs to Jimmy and the Navajo Nation Police. I haven't shared that one with the FBI."

"Where was Jimmy all this time?" Eagle Feather asked.

"I called him right away, he got there right after the state troopers. He stayed on after I took my family away from there. Which reminds me, I need to check in with him." Zack pulled out his phone. He saw there was a message from Jimmy. He listened to it.

Linda watched Zack's face. "What is it?"

"Jimmy's on his way to the Tuba City Health Care Center. An ambulance transported Naatnish there this morning. He was complaining of chest pain."

CHAPTER FORTY-ONE

Zack's phone rang. It was Jimmy.

"Zack, you got my message?"

"Yeah. What's going on?"

"I'm in the lobby at Tuba City Regional Health Care. I can't get any information on Naatnish except he is in critical condition. They won't let me in until his condition is stabilized."

"Has he got any family?"

"I didn't think so. I claimed to be a nephew when I got here, figured I could get in that way. It backfired. Someone claiming to be his sister is with him. She told the nurse not to let me in. But that's not why I called."

"Oh?"

"I just got a call from the receptionist at the facility where Nate lives. She said she didn't know who else to call."

"About what?"

"They hauled Nate out of there by ambulance early this morning. She was concerned he didn't have things he needed, like wallet, med cards and stuff, so she went to his room to check. She found a hand towel in the bathroom with blood on it. When she checked his closet, she noticed a rucksack against the back wall holding what looked like his cane. She pulled it out and found herself holding a fibula. She went for the porter; together they pulled the bag out. You can probably guess what they found."

Zack groaned. "A skull."

"Yup, they found a child's skull with half the back missing and several other bones. That's when she called me. I told them you'd be right there."

"Jimmy, keep an eye on Nate. I'll get a guard assigned to his room."

"Don't worry, Zack. That guy isn't going anywhere."

Zack put away his phone. He looked at Linda. "Don't go anywhere. There's a lot more stuff coming in."

Linda made a face at the word "stuff", but Zack wasn't watching. He turned to Eagle Feather. "Come on. We've got some old bones to pick up over at Hopi Assisted Living."

They took Zack's pickup and were there in five minutes. The receptionist greeted them at the door, introduced herself as Nancy. She led them down a shiny corridor to Nate's room.

"What's he like as a resident?" Zack asked.

Nancy gave him a soft smile. "He's a sweet man. He doesn't communicate well, though, keeps to himself. People can get the wrong idea about him."

"What's he doing in this facility?"

"Nate has a heart condition. He experiences flutters occasionally that incapacitate him. And he's got a touch of Alzheimer's; we lose him from time to time."

Zack and Eagle Feather exchanged glances.

The girl ushered them through the door to Nate's room. The porter was already there.

"After we found all those bones, we put everything back where we found it," he said.

Zack nodded. "Good work."

The room space was small for a suite, but larger than a motel room, with a divided living and bedroom area, a sink and a counter with a hot plate. The girl explained that the residents used a common dining area. Paintings of Hopi pueblos adorned the wall.

Nancy pointed to a built-in closet. "The bag is in there. The thing on the floor is the bone I thought was Nate's cane." She gave a shudder.

Eagle Feather went to the closet. Zack looked around. "Where's the hand towel with the blood you found?"

"It's on the bathroom counter," she said.

Zack put on plastic gloves, took a large Ziploc from his kit and went into the bathroom. He picked up the hand towel by a corner, inserted it into the bag. After a look around, he returned to the living room. He glanced at Eagle Feather, who was kneeling at the closet, peering into an open rucksack.

"These are old bones," the Navajo said. "They might have been dug out of a grave. Many of them have caked dirt in the cracks."

Zack leaned over to look. He grunted, walked away a few steps. He called Jimmy; his eyes scanned the room as he spoke. "We've got everything here as you described. I'm gonna take the bloody towel and bones over to Linda at the lab, if that's okay with you."

"Yeah, that's fine," Jimmy replied. "Do me a favor, seal the apartment off. I need to give the Hopi Rangers a chance to go over it."

Zack tossed a pair of plastic gloves at Eagle Feather. "Bring the bag of bones along. Jimmy will liaison with the Hopis." He went into the bedroom, studied it, noticed the absence of any family photos, or personal belongings. He asked Nancy about that.

"Yes, usually the walls of Alzheimer's patients are full of family photos, like reminders, you know? Nate never had any, he doesn't have any family."

"Lieutenant Chaparral says there's a sister with him in critical care right now."

Nancy looked surprised. "I never heard of a sister."

Zack pulled out his phone again. "Jimmy, you may want to check the bona fide of that sister."

Eagle Feather was at the sink next to the hot plate. "There's a knife here, looks like there might be blood on it, and a sliced apple in the sink. Maybe Nate cut his finger, wiped it on that towel."

"We'll run tests on the towel and the knife." Zack took out another zip-lock. "Bring it along."

They went out the door. After Nancy locked it, Zack put tape across it. The porter said he would keep an eye on the door until the Hopi Rangers arrived.

Zack put the bag of bones and his kit behind the seat of the pickup. Before he turned the key, he looked at Eagle Feather and shook his head. "I just don't get the

192

feeling from that room it's the same guy who raised hell at my ranch last night."

Eagle Feather cocked an eyebrow at him. "Here is a man we know has been to your house once already, acted suspiciously, lied to Libby about his purpose there, and ends up in the hospital this morning with a chest problem. Now we find a bloody towel and a bunch of bones in his room, and you say it doesn't feel like it's him. How much evidence do you need, White Man?"

"Well, you put it that way, it's rather compelling."

"Rather."

Zack started the truck. The men rode silently the three miles to the FBI office. After he pulled up to the curb, Zack killed the engine, but didn't move.

"What's the biggest question in your mind right now?" he asked Eagle Feather.

The Navajo didn't hesitate. "I'd like to know more about Nate's chest problem."

Zack nodded in agreement. "That one is pretty near the top of my list, too. I'd also like to know about this sister who came out of the woodwork. Then I'd like to know what happened to Emma, and where Amå is buried. I'd like to know what the mountain lion's got to do with any of this. And I'd really like to know why this killer is so interested in my house and not, say, yours?"

"You've got a lot of questions, White Man."

Zack gave a tight smile. "Yeah, I do. Let's go get this stuff to Linda. Maybe her tests will shed some light on things."

CHAPTER FORTY-TWO

Linda's Lab was like a sauna compared to the brisk outdoor temperature. The forensics expert was reading something off her computer screen when Zack and Eagle Feather arrived.

"Hey, your timing's right on, boys. I just got a DNA report on those hair samples."

Eagle Feather looked at Zack.

Zack explained. "I took some hair samples from a hair brush in Emma's house. I had no warrant, it won't stand up in court as evidence one way or the other, but I figured it might give us a lead." He looked at Linda. "What did you find?"

She looked at him with a strange expression. Zack didn't like it when Linda looked at him with strange expressions—it never boded well.

"There is no match for the hair samples in the FBI criminal database, nor in the Navajo Nation Police criminal database, which I ran at the same time."

"So, nothing."

"I didn't say that. Just for jollies, I ran it through the law enforcement agency employee DNA database. I got a match."

Both men asked, "Who?"

Linda's grin was pure evil. "You, Zack."

Zack's jaw dropped. "How...?" He was flummoxed. "I missed my hairbrush, I figured I just misplaced it. The hairbrush in Emma's bathroom looked familiar, but I thought nothing of it. How could my hairbrush get to Emma's house?"

"You took hair from your own hairbrush for me to analyze," Linda said, staring at Zack. "I'm not that desperate for work."

Zack gave Linda a bemused look. "Were all the samples a match for my hair?"

She nodded, her smile widening.

"What got into your head to check the law enforcement database?" Eagle Feather asked.

She shrugged. "I learned long ago not to discount the guys who uphold the law."

"Cynic."

Zack was barely listening to them. He slumped onto a stool. "So this so-called witch is really trying to harm me. Is it Emma? My hairbrush was at her house."

"Who could have access to your hairbrush? Where do you keep it?" Eagle Feather asked.

Zack gave a slow shake of his head. "It stays at my house, in my bathroom." A thought crossed his mind. "Wait a minute." He grabbed his phone, dialed Libby's room number at the Grand Hotel.

"Hi, Libby, it's Zack. Are you two okay? Yeah, I'm fine. I have a question for you. When Naatnish came to the house, did he ever go anywhere near the bathroom?" He listened as she described the visit. "He did, then. Yeah, it may be important. I'll call you soon. Thanks. Love you. Bye."

Zack eyed Eagle Feather. "Nate borrowed the bathroom during his visit to my house."

Before Eagle Feather could respond, Zack's phone rang. He picked it up. He listened, put the phone away.

"That was Jimmy. Nate is dead. The sister has vanished. He says we'd better get over there."

Jimmy was waiting for them in reception when Zack and Eagle Feather strode through the doors of the Tuba City Health Care Center. Zack saw right away he was mad as hell.

"I don't believe it. The hospital staff refused to let me near that room, now the sister is gone and Nate is dead."

"Didn't you post a guard?"

Jimmy glared at Zack. "I asked for one, but he hadn't arrived yet. I have to ask nicely, you know. I don't run the Tuba City police. He's here now, a bit late. Anyway, I was right here all morning. There's the elevator, right there. That door over there leads to the stairs. I've got it covered."

"No rear fire escape?"

"Sure there is, but it's alarmed—I'd have heard it. Besides, Nate was in no condition to go anywhere, according to the nurses. I wasn't overly worried about it."

"Whoa, Jimmy, no one's blaming you. Can we go up and see him?"

"I'm the one blaming me," Jimmy said. "Yeah, follow me." He led them to the elevator.

Jimmy pushed the button for the second floor. "Know what his heart complaint was? Turned out it was a heart attack; just a simple heart attack." Jimmy was still seething.

"Is that what killed him?"

"No. I'll let you see for yourself."

When the elevator door opened, Zack saw a burly Navajo Nation policeman in the corridor. They walked past him and into the room. Nate lay on his back on the hospital bed. A spider's web of tubing and wires looped from his head, arm, and chest on their way to bottles and machines that glowed and hummed. None of it would do any good now. The handle of a large knife protruded from the middle of Nate's chest.

"Damn." Zack stared. A chair was next to the bed, arranged as for a visitor, the so-called sister no doubt. There was little room for anything else in the room, with all the critical care machinery.

"Where's the nurse?" Eagle Feather asked.

"Naatnish had stabilized. The critical care nurse was in and out, so was the doctor. The nurse came in when the monitors straight-lined," Jimmy said.

"The sister was gone?"

"Yeah."

Zack leaned over the body, noted the placement of the knife. "He must have died right away after the knife entered his chest. The sister wouldn't have had much time to escape. Did the nurse notice anyone in the corridor?"

"She doesn't remember seeing anybody."

197

Zack pushed his hat back, gripped his chin. "Jimmy, let's share forensics on this too. Your Tuba City colleagues will get prints and do a sweep in here, right? Would you send copies of the results to Linda?"

"Yes, of course."

"What's the name of the nurse? I'd like to ask her a few questions."

"Her name is Katy. She's the tall one, slender, brown eyes, attractive."

Zack gave Jimmy a quick look. "I'll be at the nurses' station, then." He went out into the corridor, found the desk. The nurse looked up at his approach. Attractive, big brown eyes. Jimmy was right.

"Are you Katy?"

She nodded, smiled. "How can I help you?"

"Zack Tolliver, FBI." He rolled out his badge. "I'd like to ask you a few questions."

She nodded, brown eyes earnest.

"Were you here when the alarm sounded for Mr. Featherman?"

She nodded again.

"When you ran into Mr. Featherman's room, did you see anyone else?"

She shook her head. "No. His sister was gone. The room was empty."

"You found him as he is now, with the knife in his chest?"

"Yes." It was almost a whisper.

"What did you do?"

198

"I buzzed for the doctor, waited for him to arrive. I didn't dare touch the knife, but I knew Mr. Featherman was dead. When the doctor arrived, I asked if I should call the police. He sent me down to find Lieutenant Chaparral in the lobby."

"So you..."

"I went down to the lobby and brought him up."

"Okay, Katy, these next questions are very important. Please think carefully before you answer."

Katy nodded, her face rapt.

"First question. When the cardiac monitor alarm sounded and you responded, did you see anyone in the corridor?"

"No."

"Katy, this is very important. You're sure you didn't see anybody, not even hospital staff?"

"Oh, yes. I didn't think you meant staff. I believe there was a staff member at the far end of the corridor."

"You didn't see who it was?"

"No, no, I just saw the white coat. My mind was on the patient. The staff person was walking away, I didn't pay attention."

Zack smiled at her. "There, you see? You saw more than you thought you did. Was that person male or female?"

"Oh...I think male."

"Do you know all the men who work here?"

"I believe so."

"Okay, we'll play a game. It's important you not think before you respond—just say the first answer that comes to mind. Are you ready?"

She nodded, eyes a little wider.

"Was the man you saw a doctor?"

She paused, blurted, "Oh, no, couldn't have been. We only have two in today. I knew where both of them were."

"That's fine. Was that man a male nurse?"

She shook her head. "No, not on this floor. Besides—"

"Remember, just answer yes or no. Was he an orderly?"

"No, yes, uh, maybe..."

"That pretty much covers it, but we'll go with "no". Last question, was the man a stranger?"

"Yes." Her eyes widened more than seemed possible. "Yes, you're right, he didn't belong to the staff. I didn't recognize his back."

"Thank you, Katy. You did really well."

Later, after the Navajo Nation Police Forensics team sealed off the room, Zack, Eagle Feather and Jimmy went down to the lobby to exchange information. They grouped a sofa and a chair and sat.

"Did you ever get to see this sister?" Zack asked Jimmy.

He shook his head. "No. They wouldn't let me near the room, said the sister was very insistent."

CAT

"I don't think it was a sister," Zack said. "I don't even think it was a woman. Katy saw someone in a white coat walking away at the far end of the corridor. She thought it was a strange male."

"You think the killer was pretending to be the sister?" Eagle Feather eyed Zack.

"Yes, I do."

Jimmy shook his head. "That person sat in the room all morning long claiming to be Nate's sister, with doctors and nurses coming and going, even spoke to the doctor, at least enough to keep me out of there. How could a guy pull that off?"

"I don't know," Zack said. "I suppose a concerned relative, wrapped in a shawl or whatever, head down most of the time, back to the door might escape hard scrutiny. The doctor's mind is on his emergency, his eyes on the patient, not the visitor. When questioned, he shakes his head, disguises his voice if he must speak, and uses single syllables. He might fool very busy nurses and doctors. The beauty of it is, dressing as a woman might help him escape. Everyone knows a woman was in the room, no one's thinking about a man when he walks away."

Eagle Feather cocked an eyebrow at Zack. "Not bad, White Man. What did he do with the woman's clothes he wore in there?"

"He might have worn some sort of a loose tunic with a shawl over his head. All he has to do is drop the shawl and throw on a white orderly's jacket. He could have found one of those in a closet on the way in, hid it under the tunic." Zack raised his palms. "It would be difficult, require a lot of hubris, but not impossible."

After a moment, Jimmy nodded. "I think you are right. We are looking for a man."

"That would appear to let Emma off the hook, except for the question of how your hairbrush got into her house," Eagle Feather said. "Unless someone planted it there to misdirect us. If so—"

Zack finished his thought. "If so Emma is probably dead."

CHAPTER FORTY-THREE

"What now, White Man? I think you just ran out of suspects."

"If we are right about this," Jimmy said.

"Maybe that knife handle will have some big juicy prints on it," Zack said.

Eagle Feather grinned at Zack. "I'll bet it does, and I'll bet they'll be yours, just like the hair."

"Yeah, the hair." Zack grew thoughtful. "The question is, how did my hairbrush get from my house to Emma's house? It seems likeliest Nate took it from my bathroom. Did he give it to someone else, or did he give it to Emma? His retirement home is just down the road from her place. Is that a coincidence? In any case, why was it there and what does someone want with it?"

"To frame you," Eagle Feather said.

"To bewitch you," Jimmy said.

Zack looked at each of them, shook his head. "Nate takes the hairbrush. He's murdered, which suggests to me someone wanted to keep him quiet. Was Nate the killer's partner? Was he an errand boy? In either case, why would Emma want the hairbrush?"

"So you haven't ruled out Emma."

"I didn't say she wasn't a suspect, just dead."

Jimmy leaned forward. "Could we be talking about a partnership, maybe even a conspiracy?"

"I don't think we can discard that possibility." Zack stood and stretched. "Maybe it's time to search Emma's house a little more thoroughly." He turned to Jimmy. "Since it's on the Hopi Reservation, it's out of your jurisdiction, Lieutenant. I'll get my office to authorize a warrant in conjunction with the Hopi. It might take a while, but I'll call you when it's ready."

Jimmy and Eagle Feather climbed to their feet. Jimmy went upstairs to consult with the forensics team at work there.

Zack and Eagle Feather drove to the FBI office, where Zack called in the warrant. Back in the lab, they found Linda arranging bones on the aluminum table. The skeleton taking shape was not large.

Linda spoke as she worked. "I can't give you much, yet. That's definitely blood on the towel; I don't know whose. As for the bones, this is a child, as we surmised, maybe 6 or 7 years old. From the skull features I'd say off hand she's Native American, definitely female. Near as I can tell, she died a natural death; I didn't find any cuts or fractures on the bones to say otherwise."

"What about that big chunk out of the back of her skull?" Zack said. "What caused that?"

Linda turned the skull so they could see it better, traced the edge of the missing area with her finger. "This was done after the bone had aged significantly. Look at the way it splinters and cracks along the edge. Someone dug up this skull and redecorated it." She went back to arranging the skeleton, humming Dry Bones as she worked.

CAT

Zack glanced at Eagle Feather. "I'll bet this skeleton came from the old Mormon cemetery."

"What makes you think so?"

"Jimmy and I found a place where someone dug up a small grave. Likely it came from there. The question is, did Nate dig it up? If not, how'd it get into his closet? And why dig it up at all?"

Eagle Feather shook his head. "There can only be one reason to dig it up. You just don't want to believe it." He lifted a tiny tibia, looked at it. Linda slapped his hand. He put it down, went on. "Someone wanted to make corpse powder. They needed a child, and they wanted the bone from the back of the skull."

"Do you think Nate was making corpse powder? Does that make him a skinwalker? If so, he's a dead one."

Linda looked up. "Maybe someone would like us to think Nate was a skinwalker. That would allow the real skinwalker to go on about his business." She grinned. "You know, skin walking." She went back to work, resumed humming.

The men stared at her.

"Someone might also want us to believe Emma was a witch," Eagle Feather said, after a moment.

"We need that warrant," Zack said.

It took several more hours for the red tape to unravel. Linda kicked the men out of her lab long before that, promising she'd call if and when she had something new to report. Zack went over to Julia's Diner to have a blueberry pie moment. Eagle Feather curled up in his truck and took a nap.

CHAPTER FORTY-FOUR

Jimmy Chaparral hung around on the second floor at the hospital longer than absolutely necessary. Katy, the very attractive nurse, was still on duty. He found her brown eyes on him a few times when he looked her way.

Despite that, he felt like a fifth wheel. The two policemen with the Tuba City forensics team knew what they were doing. Jimmy could only watch as they worked the room. Nate's body was gone by now, off to Flagstaff for the medical examiner to have a look. The critical care floor supervisor hung about, anxious to get her room back.

The more Jimmy thought about it, the more he thought Zack might be wrong, and Emma was the real killer. She was the only true suspect they had, to his mind, the only person with motive and opportunity. After all, she studied healing with Amå. It was not a huge step from healing to witchcraft. No one had seen her since Amå's murder—to Jimmy, that was suspicious.

He was glad Zack suggested they search her home. The problem was the delay caused by the long wait for a search warrant. If she suspected they were this close, as she likely did, she'd remove all evidence—remove herself, for that matter.

He excused himself from the forensics squad. His mind was made up to begin the search now. His plan was delicate, the jurisdiction fragile. A Navajo cop found in a Hopi house illegally could cause awkward moments. He'd get in touch with Danny first; tip him off so the former Hopi Ranger could cover for him if he was discovered.

Jimmy parked the Blazer directly in front of Emma's house. There was no point in pretense. Next he placed a call to Danny, to explain what he had in mind.

Danny was easy with it. "No problem, Jimmy. I know a girl on the police switchboard, I'll have any calls related to a disturbance at Emma's house relayed to me first."

With mounting excitement Jimmy grabbed his flashlight, holstered it next to his handgun. He climbed out of the truck and went to the front door. He knocked, got no response. He wasn't surprised. He tried the door. It was locked. That was a surprise. Jimmy remembered it had been open his last visit.

He walked around the side of the house, touched the hood of the Chevy pickup as he passed. Stone cold. It hadn't gone anywhere. The back porch steps creaked under his weight, the small porch rang hollow under his feet. He rapped on the glass with his knuckles, called out.

"Emma. It's Jimmy Chaparral."

The back door was also locked. Emma must have returned, possibly gone out again—or was inside playing possum. Jimmy's suspicions deepened.

He turned around on the porch, faced the backyard, undecided about his next move. If Emma were indeed home, an intrusion would be more than awkward. The Hopi might even see it as criminal. At the very least, the Hopi Rangers would delight in embarrassing a Navajo cop.

He stared across the back yard, more a patch of dry dirt than lawn. Whisps of straw-like grass grew in bunches. Beyond was the garden. By contrast, plants here were green, the soil looked dark and rich. Someone was caring for it. It appeared to be cultivated and watered. Recently. A row of corn served as a windbreak for a patchwork of other vegetables. A rectangle of soil had been prepared for the next planting. At the far end of the patch, more plants, a couple of pale stalks from some vegetable he didn't recognize. The back fence was overgrown with vines, perhaps a type of squash. It was a nice effect while providing privacy from the view of neighbors across the bleak terrain.

This garden must have been tended within the last 24 hours. Did that mean Emma was home? Why would tending her garden be the first think she'd do after burying her friend and mentor? Jimmy wondered if she had a neighbor who kept the garden up in her absence.

Jimmy realized he would have to wait for the warrant after all. He came down from the porch. His eye returned to the two stalk-like vegetables at the far end of the freshly tilled earth. He chuckled. They looked just like a pair of bare toes sticking up from the ground. He paused, looked again—his smile faded.

Jimmy walked over to the garden, stopped at the edge of the fresh earth. The two objects were five feet away now. They were definitely not vegetables; they were toes. He stared, thought about where he stood, stepped back and looked at the loose dirt at his feet. He knelt down, scooped the dirt away with his hands. A nose, face, the dead eyes of Emma Truewoman appeared.

Jimmy rocked back on his heels, stunned. His instincts had served him well. The killer was erasing his tracks, eliminating witnesses: first Amå, then Nate, now Emma. He knew why. Each of the victims could identify him; they all knew him.

His eyes swept over the garden, the fresh green of nurtured plants, the vine strangling the rails. The smell of damp earth filled his nostrils. A magpie scolded. A strange calm came over him.

He knew who the killer was.

The afternoon sun behind Jimmy cast his squatting shadow across Emma's dirt-smeared face. A longer shadow grew beyond his. Jimmy started to rise, felt a blow to his head. His world went dark.

CHAPTER FORTY-FIVE

Zack knelt by Jimmy Chaparral's motionless body, felt for his carotid artery, and put his cheek next to Jimmy's mouth. He felt warmth, but very little actual breath.

"He's still alive, but barely."

Eagle Feather had placed an emergency call for an ambulance as soon as they found Jimmy's prostrate body.

It was Eagle Feather who spotted movement when they drove up to the house, something large going over Emma's back fence. Zack had turned his head in time to see what looked like the end of a long tail.

The two men ran to the back of the house. They found Jimmy on his back, his legs askew, his scalp lacerated and red with blood.

They waited next to him for the ambulance. Eagle Feather put his vest across Jimmy's torso. Zack supported him to help him breath. He stared at the scalp wound. "It's almost as if someone scraped the back of his head with a pitchfork."

Eagle Feather's response was emphatic. "Or a mountain lion swiped him with his claws. I saw one go over the back fence."

"I couldn't be sure." Zack shifted his weight; his leg had fallen asleep. "What I saw was either a large tail or a thick length of rope."

"It was a mountain lion."

"Right here among all these houses," Zack said, questioning.

"Mountain lions can and often do wander into neighborhoods like this. I know it seems unlikely, with so many dogs around. But remember, we're not talking about just any lion."

They heard the siren a few blocks away. Eagle Feather went out to guide the truck in. The driver brought the ambulance right across the lawn into the back yard.

Zack and Eagle Feather stood back, watched the attendants slide Jimmy onto a board, lift him into the ambulance. An attendant handed the vest back to Eagle Feather. In moments the vehicle was gone, lights flashing, siren sounding.

Eagle Feather walked back to where they had found Jimmy, right at the edge of the garden. His gaze went to the soft dirt beyond. He walked over there, stared down.

"We need to make another call," he said.

Zack came over and looked. "So. The mysterious Emma." He knelt, brushed away some dirt. "I think we can officially rule her out as the killer. Looks to me like she's been here a couple of days."

"Why do you think Jimmy come here before we got the warrant?"

"He was impatient. I think he was convinced Emma was the skinwalker." Zack scraped away more dirt, exposing her throat. Even through the dirt he could see the ugly bruising on her neck. "Looks like she got the same treatment as Amâ."

He sighed, stood, took his cell phone from his pocket. First he called the Navajo Police, next the Hopi Rangers. Finally he called Linda, explained the situation to her.

"Linda, I need you to get a look at this body somehow without offending either the Navajo or Hopi. I've offered our services to both. I want to know if Emma's death can be tied to the same killer."

Linda gave a chuckle. "Don't worry, Zack, I'm good at worming my way into places I'm not wanted."

Eagle Feather had gone to the far end of the garden, where he studied the ground.

Zack went to join him.

Eagle Feather raised his eyebrows at Zack, pointed to a clear footprint of a very large mountain lion. There were more. It had stood there, apparently, taking its time. Deeper imprints showed where it had sprung up and over the fence as Zack's pickup approached.

Beyond Emma's backyard the terrain reverted to sparse, arid land. Here the ground was hard; they could find no sign at all.

The Navajo and the FBI agent stood side by side, stared off across the barren landscape.

"He wanted us to see him," Eagle Feather said. "He waited. He could easily have gone before we pulled up."

"You talk about it like it's a person, not a cat."

Eagle Feather didn't answer.

"We'll get him, " Zack said.

Eagle Feather hoisted an eyebrow. "You've got a plan, White Man?"

"I asked Linda to get involved. If she can find forensic evidence to tie Emma's murder to whoever or whatever killed Amå, or to the blood sample from whoever attacked my family, the FBI can take full jurisdiction."

"How?"

"The murderer will have crossed national borders, Navajo and Hopi."

"You think she can match it? Even if it's animal DNA?"

"She'll need to wheedle samples away from either the Navajo or the Hopi. Then she'll need to send them to a really good lab." Zack turned to Eagle Feather with a grin. "My bet is on Linda."

CHAPTER FORTY-SIX

Katy answered the phone when Zack called the Tuba City Health Care Center where the ambulance had taken Jimmy Chaparral. He was in critical but stable condition, she said, drifting in and out of consciousness.

She read the doctor's notes to Zack.

"Damage to the cerebrum, particularly the temporal lobe and to the forward region of the parietal lobe. Extent unknown. Further exploration required."

"He tried to speak when he first arrived, but his words made no sense," Katy said.

"Any thoughts on what he might have been trying to say?"

"He kept repeating a word like "coat" or "moat" or something like that. The doctor said not to read anything into his words; damage to the temporal lobe can sometimes scramble language. The patient will mean to say one thing, but something entirely different comes out."

"Any prognosis?"

"It's too early yet. He's going in for exploratory surgery soon, we'll know more after that."

Zack sighed as he rang off, looked at Eagle Feather. His friend watched him, his hands wrapped around a coffee cup. He'd gotten the gist of the conversation.

As expected, Linda found no fingerprints on the knife handle. The knife itself was a common souvenir knife sold at local gift shops; even the hospital shop carried them.

Linda kicked the men out of the lab again, saying she couldn't tell them anything until all the tests came back. They'd already been kicked out of the hospital, so they ended up in Julia's Diner one more time.

Zack put away his phone, answered Eagle Feather's inquiring look. "The good news, they've got him stabilized. Bad news, they don't know when he'll be able to talk and make sense."

Eagle Feather sipped his coffee, stared at the cup. "Why try to kill Jimmy?"

"He found Emma's body."

"So did we. Sooner or later someone had to find it. It's got to be more than that. Jimmy must know something—maybe some facts came together for him. Whatever it was, it took him to Emma's house, to his discovery of Emma's body somehow. The killer must have known he had the information."

Zack considered that, nodded. "He must have collected those final pieces recently, otherwise the killer would have acted sooner. Besides, Jimmy would have told us. This feels like a desperate act."

"Yes, I agree. He would have told us what he knew. What could he possibly know that we don't? All three of us were together at the hospital; we shared all our information right there in the lobby. What did Jimmy learn after that?"

CAT

Zack rubbed his finger on the edge of his water glass. "Maybe it was after you and I left the hospital. Jimmy hung out there a while, Katy said. Then he left, rather abruptly. The warrant came back quicker than expected, we went right to Emma's house. I don't think Jimmy had time to go anywhere else."

Eagle Feather spun on his stool to look at Zack. "Somebody knew he was going there. He must have told somebody."

"Not anyone in the hospital room. Someone in the lobby, maybe?"

"Maybe, or he called someone."

"But he didn't tell either of us. If he learned something important, I think Jimmy would have called us. I think he didn't know what he knew right then, hadn't put it together."

"You're not a Navajo, so you wouldn't think of this. If I was on my way to search a Hopi home without a warrant, or even with one, I'd be damn sure to cover my backside with somebody at that reservation."

Zack stared at Eagle Feather, slid off his stool. "Let's go check Jimmy's phone."

They drove to the hospital. A guard detail was assigned to Lieutenant Chaparral 24 hours a day until the murderer was caught. The Navajo policeman at Jimmy's door permitted them to go through his personal effects.

"You catch that bastard."

They found his cell phone and checked his calls. None were unexpected for that day—calls to Zack and

Eagle Feather, several to the Tuba City Navajo police, a few to members of the forensics team.

His last call had been to Danny Kykotsa.

"He met up with this guy earlier," Zack said.

Eagle Feather knew Danny. "He's an ex-Hopi Ranger, a friend and confidant. Jimmy often checked with him about Hopi affairs."

"Has he known him long?"

"Several years, at least."

"That's it, then," Zack said. "He's the guy Jimmy called to clear the way for his search. Danny knew he was about to search Emma's house."

"Danny might have mentioned it to someone."

"Whatever, we start with Danny." Zack gave Jimmy's phone back to the guard, looked at Eagle Feather. "Do you know where Danny lives?"

Eagle Feather shook his head. "Never met the man. I only know about him because Jimmy talked about him."

Zack called his office, asked Alex Brown to do a vehicle registration search for one Danny Kykotsa and get an address. It wasn't long before Alex called back.

"Got it," Zack said. He put his phone away. "He lives just outside Moenkopi, south off Tewa Drive road. Right down by the river basin. I've got the GPS quadrants."

"Let's go."

They took Zack's pickup. On Tewa Drive road they rolled past the turnoff to Emma's house.

Zack glanced at Eagle Feather. "Another coincidence?"

"Moenkopi isn't that large. Everyone lives close to everyone else."

The road twisted and turned through neighborhoods before it settled on a direction—south. They left the houses behind, came into cropland and continued several miles toward the river. Where the terrain dropped town to the river, the road swung west following the river bench. Shortly thereafter, a lesser road branched south into the basin. Zack lurched to a stop, checked the GPS.

"This is it." He looked down the road to where it disappeared, raised an eyebrow at Eagle Feather. "You armed?"

The Navajo shook his head.

"Take my rifle."

Eagle Feather lifted the 30-30 from its rack, checked the load and rested the rifle stock downward between his legs.

Zack turned down the road. It ran beside an irrigation ditch toward the river. He slowed as the truck approached a grove of cottonwoods. A house peered out from among the trees.

Zack checked the GPS again. "That's not it. The road should turn soon."

It did, an abrupt zag west. Now they saw fields below them, on terraces. The road swung south a final time, headed straight toward the river.

Zack glanced at the GPS. "The next house should be it."

The road was potholed, the pickup bounced hard. Zack slowed. They mounted a slight rise. Several buildings came into view below them, tucked into a copse of trees next to the river. A traditional hogan nestled among them. Smoke rose above it.

"No chance to creep up on him from here," Eagle Feather said. He indicated the dust rising behind them. The truck rattled and banged, despite the slower speed.

The Navajo kept his hand on the door handle. "If he shoots, I'm gonna bail. We can divide his attention."

Zack nodded, his eyes on the trees.

There was no shot.

They drove in slow, an easy target, feeling vulnerable. The road was no more than ruts now.

"Don't see anyone down here."

"Wouldn't see him if he wanted to shoot us," Eagle Feather said.

"Thanks for that thought."

The road made a final swing east into the trees and neared the hogan. A figure came through the door, sat on the stoop, rifle cradled across the knees.

Zack kept coming at a crawl.

A hundred feet away, Eagle Feather slipped out the truck, walked away at an angle, the rifle loose at his side.

Zack inched forward, stopped fifty feet away. He stepped out of the truck, faced the hogan, his hand resting easy on the holstered sidearm.

An old woman stared back at him. She had bushy white hair tied back, sun blackened skin, a traditional shirt to the knees cinched with a conch belt, leggings and moccasins. Old school.

"Danny Kykotsa," Zack said, not a question.

The face crinkled, smiled, and bared a few yellow teeth. It was not a welcoming smile. The old woman's face was deeply etched from age, experience, who knew what else.

"Danny said you would come." Her voice was thin and reedy. She cackled.

Zack tried again. "Where is Danny?"

Another cackle. "Not here."

"Where, then?"

Her eyes narrowed into a sly look. "He said to tell you if you want him, you'll find him at the home of the Old Ones. He said the Navajo with the feather in his hat would know where it is."

Zack thought he heard Eagle Feather mumble *shit*.

"Who are you?" Zack asked.

The hag showed more yellow teeth in a malevolent sneer. "You know me from your night terrors, white man." She rose to her feet, unsteady, the rifle a cane, turned, pushed aside the door hanging and disappeared.

Zack let out a breath. He looked at Eagle Feather. "You know where she means?"

Eagle Feather nodded, his face grim. "It appears we must go to the home of the *chindi*."

CHAPTER FORTY-SEVEN

They stopped by Eagle Feather's pickup to retrieve his pack. Along the way they stopped at Slack Jack's, asked if anyone had seen Danny travel this road before. The regulars shook their heads, said they didn't know Danny Kykotsa.

"If he came this way very often, someone would have noticed," Zack said, when they were back in the truck.

Eagle Feather gave him a sidelong look. "You assume he travels like you and me."

Zack only grunted.

They continued west. Eagle Feather pointed out the side road to Willow Creek. Zack turned in. He glanced at Eagle Feather. "You come up here much?"

"I have been here to visit Lori Welkai's family a few times and hunted up on the mesa to the east. I had never been where we are going until last night."

Zack remembered. "You haven't had much sleep."

"The nap helped. I do not get much sleep on most hunting trips. I am used to it."

"Hence your usual sparkling conversation."

Eagle Feather grunted in reply. He pointed. "There is Lori Welkai's house. The turnoff to the trail is a bit further on."

CAT

They found the turn, crossed the creek to the old picnic table, parked among the trees so the truck was less visible from above.

The men climbed out, stretched, began to organize themselves.

"Water?" Zack offered a gallon jug from the back of the truck.

"I got a bottle."

"Flashlight?"

"I have a small one. It has a strong beam."

Zack looked at the sun, about three hours from the rim, decided to pack his big torch. He extracted it from behind the seat. "You take the 30-30," he told Eagle Feather, nodding toward the rack. "I've got my Glock."

Eagle Feather reached the rifle down. He dug in his trouser pocket, brought out a handful of cartridges.

"The rifle's already loaded."

"Not with these." Eagle Feather replaced the bullets already in the chamber.

"Oh." Zack opened the glove compartment and brought out a .38 police special, checked the load, tucked the gun in his pack. "I've got my own little surprise," he said.

They were ready. Eagle Feather led the way across the barren flatland with its purple sage mixed with prickly cholla. He turned up the sloping trail.

Near the rim, the sun angled into their eyes and framed their vision with a red fringe until the trail struck north across the mesa top. The sandstone plate was sun-streaked in brilliant red-orange, their shadows walked along with them. Well-placed rocks guided them.

The high cliffs enclosing the valley below narrowed toward the gorge. Most of the river basin was blanketed in shadow. Zack glanced at his watch. "How far to the ruins?"

Eagle Feather pointed his rifle barrel toward a large break up ahead. "It is in the cliffs of that arroyo. The rock ridge beyond is where the lion disappeared."

They were close. Zack grew more watchful. They traversed the rock surface with very little noise, but did it really matter? Danny would know they were coming, would be on the lookout. They could be in his crosshairs even now.

Before they reached the head of the arroyo, Eagle Feather stopped. He pointed into a wide fissure at his feet. "This is the way." He lifted off his pack and gave Zack a lopsided grin. "I expected to be shot before now."

"I'm glad you failed to meet your expectations."

"I do not know if that is good news or bad news. Now we must go down and dig him out."

Eagle Feather went first, dropped lightly to the cave floor. Zack handed down the rifle, slid down to join him. He glanced around the grotto, took in the smooth walls, the striated shades of orange and tan. Black handprints on the far wall stood out in bold relief.

Eagle Feather spoke in his ear. "It is tricky here. We will need to rappel this section. I will set it up. You stand guard. The rappel is easy. There is a ledge twenty feet below."

"What's after the ledge?"

"There is nothing for a very long way."

"Couldn't he be waiting for us on the ledge?"

Eagle Feather grunted. "Could be. If he is, it will be difficult. I do not believe he is there. I believe he wants to draw us into the cliff dwelling where his powers are greatest."

"I feel all better now."

Zack went first. The rappel was easy, the ledge wide as Eagle Feather foretold. Zack tied the harness to the rappel rope, gave a tug, and sent it back up. He stood guard, waited. Before long both men stood on the ledge.

Eagle Feather led Zack along the narrow shelf to the base of a hand-hewn ladder. He spoke in his ear. "This is the original ladder. It held me last time. It might also hold you, White Man."

Zack helped Eagle Feather lash the rifle to his back, watched him put the small flashlight in his mouth and begin to climb. The ancient sinews stretched and creaked under his weight. He moved his feet as if the rungs were hot coals and quickly disappeared into the shadows at the top.

Zack attempted the same technique. It did not go well. The second rung snapped under his weight. He saved himself with a vise-like grip on the ladder's vertical poles. From then on he kept his weight on those supports, put little as possible on the rungs. At the top of the ladder he wiped his sweaty forehead with his sleeve.

"Nice work, White Man," came the whisper. "We might need that rung on the way out."

Zack wasn't listening. He gaped at the amazing ruin before him, the towering mud-brick walls with windows high above, the keyhole doorways along a narrow street. He could as well be in a hilltop village in Italy.

He followed Eagle Feather along the passageway. They passed doorways framed in wood rough-hewn from piñon pine. By the light of his torch Zack saw interior walls plastered smooth, untouched by time. He had never seen such an undisturbed ruin.

Eagle Feather read his thoughts, whispered, "I think the residents are still here." He pointed his beam at a set of moccasin prints coming and going. "Those are mine from last time."

"No lion prints," Zack whispered back.

Eagle Feather shook his head. His light beam searched along the dirt pathway.

When they came to the plaza, the men directed their beams into every nook and cranny. Other passages led off among buildings that rose all the way to the cave roof. The centerpiece of the plaza was the sloped kiva. The top gaped, the opening surrounded by splintered wood.

Zack was about to comment when Eagle Feather grabbed his arm, put a finger across his lips.

CAT

Zack stood, listened. The stillness was absolute, an almost audible quiet. Then came the sound of voices, distant, indistinguishable—murmurs in low ghostly tones.

CHAPTER FORTY-EIGHT

Zack turned a slow circle, played the torch on walls, doors and windows. The whispering sound was everywhere, yet nowhere. When he concentrated on it, the sound was gone, but returned once his attention went elsewhere.

"Those are the voices of the spirits of the people who once lived here, it is their *chindi*" Eagle Feather said.

"They are the sounds made by wind currents when the outside heat meets the cool air of the cave," Zack said.

"Suit yourself, White Man."

"I see no signs of Danny in here, no tracks, not even lion tracks. Wasn't it here that you saw the mountain lion?"

"I was in that kiva, it walked above me, right about there." He directed the small flashlight beam like a pointer.

Zack circled the kiva, inspecting the ground. On the far side he found mountain lion prints, right where Eagle Feather indicated. They looked fresh. He saw no other prints, human or animal. The paw prints came from the rear of the cave along a narrow alley between buildings, went back the same way.

Eagle Feather came to look. He studied the tracks in the light of Zack's torch.

"I thought you said it returned several times that night," Zack said.

"It did."

"I see just one set of tracks."

Eagle Feather didn't respond. Zack couldn't see his face.

They followed the tracks. The path narrowed, the building walls closed in. Zack directed his torch in each keyhole doorway. Many rooms contained tools for everyday life—grinding stones, pots, a pair of woven sandals, bone utensils—all under a layer of dust.

The cave grew more restricted. Buildings were smaller, no windows, tiny doors, likely used for storage, Zack figured. Beyond the last structure the roof height dropped. Walking became difficult.

The rear of the cave resembled a den. Zack's light shown on white objects—bones he realized, lots of bones, scattered everywhere. These bones were not relics; they were from recent kills. Lion footprints were all over the compacted dirt floor. They had come to a mountain lion lair.

Zack squatted, shown his torch around the walls. They were at a dead end. Where had the lion gone?

Eagle Feather touched his arm. "Turn off your torch."

"What? Why?"

" Just do it."

Zack did as he was asked. With the lights off, the darkness was complete. Eagle Feather's grip tightened on Zack's arm. "Leave it off for a while. Just feel, listen, use all your senses."

Zack tried. It was difficult to concentrate when he expected to feel the crushing weight of a huge lion on his back any moment. It rather spoiled the effect.

He heard Eagle Feather sniff the air. Zack drew a large breath through his nose. Now he noticed something other than the stale cave air—delicate whisps of sage and piñon. He thought he felt air move on his cheek. His eyes actually adjusted to the dark, he began to perceive stratification in the immutable blackness. He saw areas of lighter gloom, not toward the cave entrance, but deeper into the cavity. He knew now what Eagle Feather had sensed. "There's another entrance."

"Yes." Eagle Feather's whisper came in his ear. "The light comes from above somewhere."

He heard Eagle Feather crawl deeper into the narrow cranny. Zack slithered after him on his stomach, elbows and toes propelling him along. His hand found a bone. He recoiled, but went on. The lighter shade of dark became brighter, moved overhead. He was under a crack in the cave roof, a gap in the sandstone. He thought he even detected stars.

Something touched him. Eagle Feather's voice sounded next to him. "I'm going up there. Leave off your torch, let's not advertise that we are here."

Zack waited. He heard Eagle Feather shuffle forward, heard small stones dislodged, heard loud breathing as from a great effort. The light from above was blocked. Zack lay still on his stomach, his head lifted to the limits of the cave roof, face turned away from the sprinkle of dirt and dust. The sounds above him diminished, disappeared altogether. The night sky returned. Zack waited, let the stillness wash over him. The fresh air was good. He breathed in another deep breath.

A different smell came to his nose, close by, the smell of fur and fetid breath.

Sudden searing pain knifed into his left foot. He cried out. His foot was tugged, re-gripped, pulled hard. He resisted, but was dragged back, his leg jerked and tugged. Zack pushed against the dirt floor, tried to hold. The torch came out of his hand. He turned his torso to reach it, felt his shoulders press against the cave roof. He twisted hard, jammed his body between cave ceiling and floor. It held for a moment. In that second his left hand groped for the torch, found it. He reached to grasp it, was dislodged, flipped onto his back, and dragged again. He could offer little resistance now, gave up.

With both hands free, he steadied the torch on his chest, aimed it at his feet, and turned it on. A mountain lion had his foot in its huge mouth; its phosphorescent green eyes stared back into the light.

As he bounced along Zack kept the torch beam on the lion with his left hand, groped for his holstered sidearm with his right. The lion pulled faster yet, dust and dirt spurted into his face. Somehow he managed to free the pistol, brought it above his hip, extended his arm along the top of his body and fired repeatedly at those green eyes.

The reports exploded in his ears, slammed about in the confined space, ricocheted off solid ceiling and walls like a cannon ball. His eardrums were pounded as if punched, his skull vibrated. He kept firing.

Dust rose like a blizzard around him, obscured his feet. He felt a new impact on his other foot, a new pain, knew he'd shot himself. Still the beast's jaw did not relinquish its grip, the great head shook side to side. His leg felt it must come off at the hip. He fired until the Glock clicked repeatedly on the empty chamber.

He felt someone behind him now, saw the barrel of a rifle extend past him. A thunderclap sounded next to his head, a roar that left him stunned. He felt his foot come free, he stopped moving. His head pounded in waves, his hearing was reduced to a distant roar, like far away surf. Pain grew steadily in his head, his ears. The torch fell from his chest, his head dropped back to the dirt floor. He was aware of a thin beam of light passing above him.

Zack pushed himself to his elbows, peered along the beam toward his feet.

The cat was gone.

CHAPTER FORTY-NINE

The Hopi Rangers found Danny Kykotsa lying dead on the ground outside his home south of Moenkopi. A single bullet hole adorned the middle of his forehead like a medallion; most of the upper rear of his skull was blown away. The Rangers figured the old lady had killed him with her rifle, the same one she used to shoot at the policeman's vehicle when it approached. They never understood why she killed her own boy. They figured she was crazy.

They brought her in, put her in a cell. She never said a word, never interacted with anyone, just sat on the floor with her back against the wall, staring at nothing. Every once in a while the guard heard her cackle, as if she'd just thought of something funny. No one knew what to do with her, they had no evidence, no proof she had killed her son. She wouldn't eat, wouldn't move.

The morning they came to release her, they found her hanging from the cell bars. She had torn her skirt into strips, woven it into rope. It was done with patience, with the skill of ancient weavers, each over and under twist of the cloth strip precisely like the next. Then she'd used it to hang herself.

When they removed Emma's body from her back-yard garden someone noticed the soil beneath her had been disturbed. They dug down another foot, found Amå. She'd been stripped of her jewelry—they later found it buried behind Danny's house along with several jars of coins. They guessed he'd dug those up at her hogan out on the mesa. They couldn't explain, or perhaps didn't want to explain the bits of bone and skull fragments, strange herbs, animal skins, feathers, and earthen jars of strange liquids they found when they searched Danny's hogan.

Jimmy Chaparral recovered quickly, in part due to the special care lavished upon him by Katy. His full head of thick black hair eventually grew back, but couldn't entirely hide the four evenly spaced white scars on the back of his head where cat claws had dug into bone.

Prónto made a full recovery. He lavished more time on his wife and family now. His ebullient spirits hadn't suffered; he was as popular as ever in social circles. There was one change. People wondered if it was his idea or his wife's suggestion to sell his expensive hunting rifle. That sale gave an immediate boost to the family finances.

Zack spent a week in the Flagstaff Health Care Center. His left eardrum was severely damaged, requiring a tympanoplasty. The procedure was 80% successful. His damaged feet took longer to heal. The cat's huge incisor had pierced his left foot just below the ankle, ripped tendons, broke the small bones and destroyed nerves. The surgery went as well as it could, but the ankle would always be stiff, always a bit limiting. He was luckier with the other foot. The 9 mm bullet pierced between the first and second metatarsal bones missing all tendons, muscles and ligaments. A clean shot.

"I never was a great dancer," Zack joked to Eagle Feather during one of his daily visits. "Now I'll really suck."

Libby and Bernie came to see him daily. One day at Libby's request Eagle Feather took Bernie outside the room, kept him engaged by pushing him along the corridor on a hospital gurney to give his friends some privacy.

Libby loved Zack, she told him, but she'd had enough. If he expected her to raise Bernie single-handed while he was off on lecture tours or chasing criminals all over the west, she'd just as soon not have the constant anxiety over his safety. The final straw was the danger she and Bernie faced these last weeks because of Zack. She wasn't asking him to give up his career, nor was she asking out of the marriage. For the time being, at least, she needed the peace of mind that could only come from not knowing that he was in danger. She needed him to move out.

"You sure shot yourself in the foot this time," was Eagle Feather's comment after Zack told him. He was in a chair by Zack's bedside, both men munching on crème-filled donuts the nurse never would have allowed.

"You re a funny guy," Zack said.

"Where will you go?" Before he could respond, Eagle Feather blurted, "Not a lot of room in my trailer."

Zack grinned. "Don't panic. I won't interfere with your solitary lifestyle." He sighed. "Libby is right, you know. I'm practically never home. It makes more sense for me to set up space in the office. I use Linda's shower all the time anyway."

"No thought of giving up this life to be with your family?"

"Of course, lots of thought. I keep coming back to the same thing, though. I'd be restless and unhappy, and I'd make everybody miserable." He gave a wan smile. "This won't last forever. Things always change, for better or worse. I've got work to do and no one else fits my job description. It's important I help Susan with her work and continue to assist other law enforcement agencies when they come up against situations they lack the understanding to handle."

"Okay, Dudley Do-right, keep up the good work." Eagle Feather shifted in his chair. "Tell me, what have you concluded about our mountain lion? You emptied your pistol at it. I shot it just above the eyes with the rifle. Yet we found no body, no blood trail—no sign of it at all. The cat simply vanished." Eagle Feather pinned an eye on Zack. "You know what happened to Danny Kykotsa. Isn't it a remarkable coincidence the old lady shot him in the exact same place I shot the lion?"

Zack raised his eyebrows. "I know you're laying a trap for me here. Let me ask you this: did they find any other bullet wounds on Danny?"

Eagle Feather shook his head.

"Yet I emptied my gun at that lion at point blank range. The 9 mm bullets might not kill it, but they should have left marks. If you believe the cat was Danny in another form, as I suspect you do, why isn't there any evidence of my bullets?"

Eagle Feather chuckled. "There is. There's a hole right through your foot."

"Okay, you can let that go any time now."

"Won't happen, White Man." Eagle Feather said, chuckling. He grew serious. "Here's my theory, since you ask. My bullets were specifically prepared to kill a skinwalker, yours were not."

"So mine had no effect whatsoever?"

"You saw. If I hadn't come back when I did, you'd have been another set of bones in that cave."

Zack shook his head, looked at Eagle Feather. "You think Danny did it all? You think he killed those mules at the Grand Canyon, dropped the snake on me, visited my house as a wolf, tried to scare me by threatening my family, murdered the guard on my porch, killed Amå while skin walking as some sort of giant raptor, killed Emma, sent Naatnish to my house to get my hair sample, then killed him in the hospital, tried to kill Jimmy at Emma's house?" Zack gave a weak grin. "And let's not forget, tried to killed me."

Eagle Feather stared at Zack. "That's right, White Man."

"And what is your explanation for how he seemed to be in two places at one time?"

"Those distances aren't so great as the crow—or should I say the owl flies."

Zack shook his head. "I don't know what I think anymore, but I'll tell you one thing—none of that will go into my official report."

Be sure to read more of Zack Tolliver, FBI.

Other novels in the series include

THE OTHER, MESTACLOCAN, and *ZACA* (Audio

Book Available)

If you enjoyed *CAT*, consider sharing your

thoughts with other readers with a review on

Amazon.com.

(Go to Amazon.com/R-Lawson-Gamble)

Other Novels by R Lawson Gamble

THE OTHER

"The hunters noticed the circling birds against the rose-tinted sky above the rim-rock and saw where the flat rays of the early morning sun glinted on something that didn't belong there and the three of them walked that way."

What they find sends FBI Agent Zack Tolliver and his friend Eagle Feather in pursuit of a dangerous and powerful killer.